I REMEMBER YOU

HOLLY SCHINDLER

I Remember You
A Ruby's Place Novel

Published by Holly Schindler, LLC

Copyright © 2018 by Holly Schindler

Cover and interior design by Holly Schindler

Cover image by Viktor Gladkov, courtesy of Shutterstock

Uplift Snow Brushes for Photoshop by Uplift Actions, and Neon Layer Styles for Photoshop by MiksKS, both courtesy of Creative Market

Fonts: Cursive Neon Tubes by Medialoot, Mirosa by Tobias Saul, and Claxton by Mike Hill, all courtesy of Creative Market

WELCOME

to

1.

1955

RUBY looked awfully pleased with herself. She stuck her pink face into the air, striking a kind of defiant pose against the December chill as she paced, her feet leaving dainty tracks in the skiff of snow on the sidewalk. She swung some sort of bell as she walked—probably one of those ringers owners attached to entrances to announce the arrival of a new customer—back and forth, up and down, around and around.

Bell ringers of the season were usually pleasant. Melodic, even. Salvation Army red kettle volunteers smiled and carolers trilled, and their bells added a charming kind of holiday ingredient to the atmosphere. Not Ruby's bell, though. It clanged and echoed and thunked and pealed, making the kind of horrible racket that demanded her fellow shopkeepers step outside to admire her glorious work-in-progress.

I Remember You

Roy Weber, owner and sole proprietor of Weber Electronics, watched her from the doorway of his shop. The way she paraded about made his stomach churn like he'd been infected with one of those awful stomach bugs his kids were always bringing home from Sullivan Elementary.

He grunted with disgust, lighting a fresh Pall Mall. He never smoked in the store, not even during the occasional, brief mealtime lull when his shop was empty. He preferred to stand under the awning that stretched all the way from his place to the entrance of The Page Turner bookstore next door. That day, as he took his first drag, he tugged upward on the bill of his black and white plaid tweed hat, as though to give himself a more unobstructed view of the newest holiday decorations that had been added to the busiest commercial street in all of Sullivan. The stretch was adorned, as usual, with pine sprigs and wreathes and giant electric candles, with plastic candy canes and rosy-cheeked Santa faces. Last weekend, the lampposts had been embellished with bright aluminum stars. They struck Roy as some sort of strange cross between a rocket and a snowflake.

Yes, that's what he pretended he was doing: admiring the stars. In truth, he'd come outside to watch the new sign going up on the bar across the street: "Ruby's Place" in bright red neon.

Ruby red, of course. How cute.

He squinted. He didn't care much for this Ruby person who had been in the process of moving in for the past several months. She barked orders at the work crews who'd been renovating the place; she unapologetically shopped in the high-end dress section of Graham's Department Store in those full pants of hers; she pumped her own gas at the station on the corner.

What, exactly, was she trying to prove?

The door behind Roy flew open. Nick emerged, wiggling his fingers, wordlessly asking to bum a smoke.

"Ought to start charging you," Roy grumbled. Roy was a steady two-pack-a-day smoker, much to his wife's chagrin, and he didn't appreciate having to share. Then again, what addict ever did? Still, he complied, just as he always complied where Nick was concerned. He was his brother-in-law after all, and tolerating him was as good as bringing home a new hat for the Mrs.—and considerably cheaper.

"You weren't kidding about how busy you've been," Nick said, ignoring Roy's annoyance about the cigarettes.

"Never had a Christmas season like this one," Roy agreed, standing straight enough to flatten his slight paunch, his chest puffing a little more. Without his topcoat, wearing only his suit jacket, the new posture was especially noticeable.

Proud as he might be, Roy's wasn't the only business in town boasting a far better than average Christmas season. It was a good time to live in Sullivan—lots of jobs, plenty of kind faces with money to spend. *Humming*. That was a good word. In Sullivan, no Classified "Help Wanted" ad went answered. A "Here" always followed a name during roll call. Your favorite scissors were always sharp and always in the drawer where you swore you put them last. Nothing was amiss or absent or out of place.

At least, it hadn't been until the bar across the street from Weber Electronics, empty long enough for Roy to have comfortably forgotten its existence, had been purchased. By a woman, of all things.

"Seems like folks are going all out this year," Nick went on. They were—that much was true. Motorola televisions and clock radios and brightly colored record players for the kids. *Teenagers*. Such a silly word. In Roy's day, you were a boy one minute and the next day—*bam!*—you were either in the military or married and employed, toiling eight-to-five five days a week to bring home the family's paycheck. Most likely, you were not just working a job, but were already in the profession where you would spend your entire career. It was almost like these kids were interning, studying up to be adults. Where did this adolescence thing—this weird free-ride period—come from? It seemed so strange.

Almost as strange as a woman running her own business.

"Kinda nice that we always get a little bit of a breather before the crowds kick in again," Nick observed.

He was talking about the rush that started in around four and lasted until around seven. The most popular holiday shopping hours for working men. Well, except for Christmas Eve, anyway. Roy planned to be open until four in the afternoon on the twenty-fourth in order to get as many of them as he could.

"I dunno. I kinda like it when the store borders on chaos," Roy said, his grin emphasizing the crinkles around his eyes. He did, too. Weber Electronics was his playground. Besides, chaos meant more rings to the old cash register—for him, the prettiest sounding Christmas carol of all.

"Sure do appreciate you giving me the extra hours," Nick said, acknowledging the opportunity.

Roy nodded. It was still only part-time, but (again, at his wife's urging) Nick had long been his go-to man during busy seasons. Roy preferred working the store himself, but his wife complained about his long hours, saying he barely saw the kids at all. He'd promised to make it up to them in the summer. A big family vacation, using some of the extra money he was making now. They'd go someplace fancy sounding. Maybe the Poconos.

What did a man with a family do in the Poconos? He wasn't sure. But his wife had always referred to the place as her idea of the ultimate destination. Maybe the travel agency had a brochure.

"You get a good look at her yet?" Roy asked, curls of smoke swirling around his head. He flicked his gold lighter for Nick. His wife was always buying him trinkets like that. The lighter on his birthday, his Bulova watch (inscribed "Ten Happy Years") for their anniversary.

"Who?" Nick exhaled.

"Whaddaya mean, who? *Her*, her." He jutted his head in Ruby's direction.

Nick raised his eyebrows and whistled. Then said, in a tone laced with sheer awe, "She was apparently quite the dancer. Ballerina."

"How do you know?"

"I introduced myself," he beamed.

Roy grunted. "Divorced? Widow?"

"Never married. Just frugal. Managed to put aside enough to have quite the nest egg. Used it to start her own business."

"Still. How much sense does that make?" Roy asked. "A ballerina opening a bar?"

"'Bar' isn't a fair description, not really. It's not going to be some watering hole for drunks. She said it was more like a… what was that word she used?" He paused, thinking. "A supper club! That's it." For emphasis, he swept his arm to the side with an elegant flourish.

"You act like you've seen it."

"I have."

Roy frowned, growing angry. It felt like a betrayal. "She let you inside?"

"Sure. It's not like she's hiding. Linen tablecloths, crystal chandeliers, a piano. And it won't be an adult-only place. Children can come, too. Everybody dressed up in their finest. Gonna be *quite* the *sight* on Christmas Eve."

Roy twisted his face into pure undeniable revulsion.

"A supper club. You know," Nick continued, as though mistaking Roy's revulsion for confusion. "Like—the Copacabana. Apparently, she was living in New York. Think they're real popular up there."

"What'd she tell you, her entire life story? My wife gets wind of this, and she'll be poring through magazines, picking out the latest in evening gowns in order to go over there. What's some dame from New York doing opening a bar—supper club, sorry—in a place like this? Pretty small beans by comparison. What, she got a sudden itch to be the big fish in a small pond?"

"She grew up not too far from here," Nick said. "Besides, she was tired of living in the Big Apple. She had a longer career than most dancers, from the sound of it. Felt like she needed a change of pace. Come back home, you know."

"Aren't we the lucky ones."

"Not sure sarcasm suits you."

"Yeah, well, I'm still not sure a bar is gonna suit her, either. I'm not going to end up being her ally, either. Faster she gets out of here, the better."

Nick shrugged. "You ever think maybe it'd be nice to get the place shined up? Been closed forever. Back during Prohibition, they say, the place was a speakeasy. I dunno—maybe you clean that place up, the whole street winds up looking better. Maybe we get even more traffic than we already have. I wouldn't mind that, would you?"

"Still." Roy shook his head. "A woman."

"Now we're getting down to it," Nick said. "So what if her shirts button on the wrong side? Maybe she'll be good at it. Would that be bad?"

Roy grimaced. "Bet she doesn't even get it open. The way you talk, she's probably about to go broke decorating the place. Women do get distracted by shiny things, you know."

"I bet she gets it open. And on time."

"Do you? Fine. Make it official. She doesn't get it open, you take me and the wife and kids out for a four-course Christmas Eve dinner, your treat."

"And if she does?"

"Then I'll go to that place every single Christmas Eve for the rest of my life—and you can come along as my guest— on me."

"Deal," Nick agreed, and they shook on it.

2.

2018

NORMALLY, Susan Fitzweather did not venture past her front door with her hair still in pink foam curlers. But she was running late, and the coast, according to the view from her front bay window with the cardinal feeder, was very clear, indeed.

So she covered her shoulders with her husband's khaki wool topcoat, hanging, as always, on the rack by the front door, and she burst onto the front porch.

She was still in her slippers, though. Pink Isotoner ballerina slippers, to be exact, with embroidery across the toes and absolutely nothing in the way of a slip-resistant sole. Or so she found out when her foot touched the slightly ice-glazed front walk.

She could have returned for better shoes. Her ankle-length hiking boots with the red laces, for example. But she was already outside, and running ever later, so many meetings to attend at the Senior Center now that the holidays were approaching.

She simply pressed forward, creeping along with her entire lower body clenched (as though this would somehow protect her from falling).

At the edge of her driveway, she scooped up the paper. She hadn't yet finished bringing herself completely upright when she heard it: "Susan!"

She gasped, finding her neighbor, Pamela Krunk, standing maybe two feet away—dressed for the day in a green puffy winter coat and matching ski hat with giant snowflakes knitted into the pattern, full makeup, her shoulder-length dyed red hair in perfect, finished curls. She held the leash for her blond Labrador, Rufus. It was time for Rufus's morning walk. But Rufus would have to wait until Pamela talked to Susan.

In the town of Sullivan, Missouri, everyone had time to talk. Even women with rollers still in their hair. Dogs simply had to learn to be patient.

Gossip was a recognized, sanctioned sport throughout the town, with an ever-shifting title-holder; she (or he—men were regular, enthusiastic participants) with the current juiciest tidbit reigned supreme. Each fleeting champion basked in the glare of being the moment's ultimate source of knowledge of all things Sullivan.

In times past, gossip had been something of an underground, even clandestine activity, practiced in the relative privacy of living rooms, barber shops, or beneath the awning of an empty electronics store experiencing the day's lull. The last home-owned neighborhood hair salon had closed about five years ago, pushing the sport into the open and causing the turf for this never-ending tournament to spread into all corners of town—checkout lines and waiting rooms, backyard chain-link fences, and, yes, morning driveways like Susan's.

"Got to get Rufus walked in order to get downtown for a little Christmas shopping," Pamela started, ignoring her neighbor's obvious embarrassment at being caught with cold cream on her face, in her plaid flannel nightgown.

"I didn't know anyone still went downtown to shop," Susan confessed, hiking her husband's collar, hoping that it covered her rollers and knowing, at the same time, that it probably didn't.

"Yes, well, the grandkids—they want different things than I'd buy for anyone our age, of course," Pamela said. "Thought I might hit the flea market. You know—the one close to the bookstore? My twelve-year-old—you remember Michael's kid—he's into collecting old Hot Wheels."

Susan saw an opening and grabbed it. "Will you be happening by Ruby's Place, by any chance?"

For months, Ruby's Place had been the subject of the most unanswered questions, the most mystery, and the most prize-winning gossip. Once Sullivan's most popular hot spot, the old bar had closed four presidents ago and had since begun to fall into disarray—at least, until a buyer had stepped in last year, during the holiday season.

Pamela cocked her head to the side as though considering it for the first time. "You know, come to think of it, I will. Since it's right near the flea market."

"Well. I did have a very interesting conversation about that place just the other day," Susan said, raising her eyebrows for emphasis.

"Did you, now?"

"Yes. Perhaps you might come by tomorrow for coffee—after your errands are run, of course?"

Pamela smiled. "I would love to."

Susan waved, and the women parted. That night, each would compose her story in her mind—almost like a local broadcast journalist prepping to be on-air. Susan would probably practice a few lines in the bathroom mirror.

Neither of them had the full story of what was actually happening over at Ruby's Place. But like everyone else in Sullivan, they had for months gleefully joined in on the whispering of overheard morsels:

"Angela's the one who bought Ruby's. You remember her. Moved back home to try to make a go of the old bar."

"You're kidding! Why would she do that? Place has been closed for eons. Gotta be a total money pit."

"Why would Angela want to take something like that on, this late in life?"

"What's going on at Ruby's, anyway? Making any progress?"

"That place is so weird. I've heard strange mumblings about it for years."

"I used to go there when I was younger. Every single Christmas. I used to think it'd be nice if it got back open, but I really gave up hope that it would ever happen years ago. Why would Angela think she can make it work when nobody else has been able to?"

"Getting so close to Christmas. You *really* think she'll be open in time for the holiday?"

"What's stopping her? What's holding the project back?"

"Well, *I* heard…"

Little did the residents of Sullivan know, those questions, that mystery, those delectable little tidbits of information weren't about to dry up anytime soon.

The story was only going to get juicier.

3.

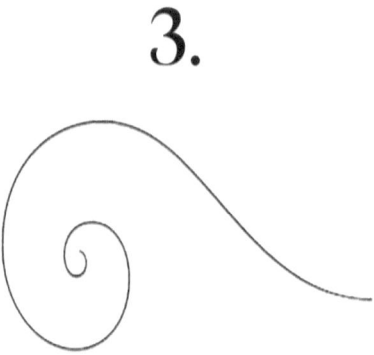

A cardinal swooped from the gray Missouri sky to land on the cold, empty sidewalk. He cocked his head, glancing up and down what had once been the busiest street in the entire town of Sullivan, as though wondering how it could be possible that here, less than a month until Christmas, his bright red feathers were the most festive decoration in sight.

To be sure, a small wreath adorned the entrance of The Page Turner bookstore. But it was looking fairly wind-tattered, frankly, with its once-strategically placed pine cones and tiny plastic ornaments all dangling loosely, threatening to tumble to the ground. The nearby diner—a tiny place that somehow managed to straddle the lines between coffee shop, sandwich shop, and convenience store—featured a sad, amateurish, hand-painted candy cane on the plate-glass window, right above the "Pastry of the Day" sign. A run-down office building, a defunct electronics store, and the Bank of Sullivan refused to acknowledge it was the holiday season at all. And Ruby's Place, the pub once considered Sullivan's crown jewel, had gotten a new coat of green paint on the front door. But then again, the front door had always been green—and couldn't be considered a purely holiday decoration.

That was all. Never, not once, had the town of Sullivan *not* adorned itself in all the twinkling, sparkling signs of the season. Even in past years, as the popularity of the downtown area had dwindled, remaining shopkeepers had still brought it upon themselves to decorate far more than they had this year.

Odd, how no one had even rented the parking lot of the now-closed gas station to sell balsam firs. No ribbons on lampposts, no strings of white lights around doorways. No animated displays, no plastic reindeer posed beneath outdoor trees, no decorative pots of poinsettias outside store entrances, not a single sign advertising cocoa with Santa. The air did not smell like pine sprigs or baked goods. Carols did not tickle the ears. Not a single shopping bag rustled as it was shoved into the trunk of a car.

This seemed to confuse the poor cardinal.

Then again, maybe that was just Angela projecting her own feelings onto the creature as she stared at him through the window of Ruby's Place.

Outside, a man in white coveralls darted in front of the window, frightening the cardinal away. He rapped on the glass, shouted, "Come take a look, boss."

It had become Angela's new nickname: boss. They all called her that—the plumbers and the electricians and the painters and the guy who'd delivered her new menus. Just the other day, when she was making her latest loan payment, she'd had to void a check for starting to write "Boss" on the line for her signature.

Angela grabbed her hat off the bar. *Uglier than sin,* those were the words her grandmother would have used to describe the stocking cap. Angela's sister had made it, though, and late last winter, she'd even started to think of it as her lucky hat, because it had been responsible for her seeing Ruby's as something much more than mold and falling plaster. That hat was, in fact, a big part of the reason why she'd bought the long-closed establishment, why she'd merrily committed to sinking her every last dime into renovations.

Earlier that very morning, she'd dragged the brown monstrosity out of her dresser drawer. Maybe, Angela'd thought, with last year's good luck charm on her head, she would find a renewed spirit of hope.

So far, though, it hadn't quite worked.

18

She hurried outside where the two workers with "Sullivan Sign & Neon" screen printed across their coveralls pointed to the ten-foot-long red vinyl strip they'd hung above the entrance.

"Looks great, guys," Angela announced, even though the impossible-to-miss "Opening Christmas Eve!" sign tied a worried knot in her stomach. That deadline was so close—and yet, inside the bar, she still had a whole construction crew working on drywall and exposed brick and vintage ceiling tile. She finally admitted to herself that she was no longer sweating bullets but giant cannonballs over whether the place would be open in time for Christmas.

And it had to be open for Christmas. Everything hinged on it.

Not that she could tell her contractors. What was she supposed to say? Something like, "Hey, guys, could you please get a move on? Because you see, this building has a secret, which I uncovered last Christmas—a magical, spiritual Christmas secret—and we've *got* to get the people of Sullivan in here on Christmas Eve to see it. Otherwise, there is a very real possibility that the place could tank. Because Christmas Eve, that's the one time of year when believing doesn't seem like a stupid thing to do. It's the one time of year when people's hearts are open to even the wildest possibilities. People believe in wishes coming true. And they'll believe in this place, too. So it has to be on Christmas Eve. Okay?"

She could only imagine how those bearded, thick-skinned, callused guys would look at her. Those guys believed in nail guns and plumber's putty. They did not believe in fairies or flying reindeer or fat men shoving presents down chimneys. They were not going to believe in ghost stories, either. Or magical bars.

"You know," one of the men told her, "it's not too late for us to get you a nice electric sign for the front—that neon restoration's awfully pricey. Those vintage signs…"

"No," Angela insisted. "I want the old one. Restored to its former glory. Like I told you. The same old neon, same old cursive letters."

"An electric sign works every bit as well, you know…"

"Some things you don't throw away," Angela said. "Some things are worth preserving."

"It's your dime…"

Both ladders rattled as they were placed back in the Sullivan Sign & Neon truck.

Angela waved goodbye, noticing that the cardinal from the sidewalk was perched on a nearby tree branch no more than five feet away.

Cardinals appear when angels are near. Angela repeated

the old saying to herself as the bitter December wind poked its fingers through the tiny holes between the stitches on her sweater. Silently, she asked that old cardinal to bring her the Guardian Angel of Contractors. Surely there had to be one. What was it about that time of year? Why did it always seem to allow even the most desperate, silly superstition to grow wings?

The clock eased toward noon, causing all the whizzing and banging to wind down inside. Overalls and paint-splattered sweatshirts paraded through the door.

"Bring you a sandwich, boss?" one of them asked, clomping his boots in the direction of the diner.

Angela shook her head, stuffing her hands into her jean pockets.

"Got a wiring snafu to talk to you about," he called.

"Wait. What? What snafu?" Angela shouted down the sidewalk.

"Talk after lunch, boss," he said with a casual wave.

In frustration, Angela grabbed the edge of her ugly hat and tugged it even farther down over her ears.

Across the street, the door to The Page Turner flapped open. Angela waved as Tom Barister stepped from the bookstore. He'd only barely nodded back when a gust hit him square in the face. His shoulders stiffened, and he tugged the collar of his coat tight around his throat. He smiled at her, his eyes surely twinkling, ready to tell her another new story, some funny anecdote. It had become their game, shortly after they'd met on that very stretch of road, during one of Tom's many book-runs: he would tell her he had a good one—a real whopper—and Angela would warn him that no matter what story he came up with, he was not going to get so much as a single snicker out of her. But he would always wind up telling her such a crazy tale that she'd burst into a round of honest belly laughter. The kind that would make her stomach sore.

She liked Tom. Usually. But after the last vague wiring warning, she was suddenly and decidedly not in the mood.

Another of Angela's many workers reached through the open passenger side window of his truck, removing a thermos and a brown bag. He poured coffee into the thermos lid, took a sip and announced, "Nothing like eating outside once it turns cold." He flipped an empty bucket upside down, with the obvious intention of turning it into a lunch seat.

"Hey," he said, "look at that."

Tom Barister had grown close enough, at this point, to hear the contractor. And to see what he was pointing at—a bold message carved long ago into what had otherwise become a cracked and aging sidewalk:

Rob & Geena 4Ever 1987

Tom seemed to forget the cold, releasing his hold on

his coat collar. Angela knew that look on his face. One of his stories had just bubbled up to the surface.

4.

1989

CHRISTMAS Eve snow trickled through the air, dancing across the windshield of Rob's Chevy.

It was a wreck of a car. The kind that only an eighteen-year-old could feel pride in owning. With nearly two hundred thousand miles racked up on the odometer, the '73 Caprice came complete with broken springs in the seats and a sun-cracked dash and rust on the bumpers. Still, Rob joked about how much he liked the mangled grille he'd mowed six thousand yards and flipped eight million McDonald's burgers and sold who-knew-how-many grosses of Independence Day bottle rockets to buy. The dented-in grille made the car look menacing. It had character. Maybe even gave Rob some character by extension. What wasn't there to like about that?

24

And besides, the Caprice provided a place where he could spend time alone with Geena. The thing had more room than most first apartments. The two of them could park along the side of any road in Sullivan, Missouri, turn the radio on, and dissolve into each other.

That night, Rob had managed to wrench her away from her mother and step-father, smuggling her out through the kitchen door. They hadn't gone far—in fact, they were parked one block over, still in Geena's neighborhood. All around them, garage doors and front yard trees had been decorated with twinkling multi-colored lights. He figured he had fifteen minutes tops before her mother started calling for her, stomping up the stairs to her bedroom, asking if she was sure she didn't want to join her and Greg for their annual viewing of *It's a Wonderful Life*.

It wasn't much, fifteen minutes. But he couldn't help himself. He had an eleventh-hour gift for her.

"You've given me a hundred presents already. What is this? Should I be braced for bad news?" Geena teased, twisting in the passenger seat to face Rob. As she moved, her right knee poked out from the hole in her acid washed Palmetto jeans.

But a hundred wasn't enough. Not for Rob. Because this would be the last Christmas before the world ripped them apart—sending Geena to college and Rob to the military.

I Remember You

He twisted the radio dial, stopping on the familiar sound of an acoustic guitar. It didn't matter that it was a new single, and that his go-to station had been playing it every time he'd flicked on the radio for about the past month. Skid Row was Geena's current favorite band, and "I Remember You" was her favorite song on their album, and with everything going on around them, it felt absolutely providential that it would be playing now.

He turned up the sound—only a little, the song would get louder with the chorus, he knew—and in the midst of all those lyrics sung by a man asking not to be forgotten, he handed Geena a small jewelry box.

Geena shredded the paper and let loose a genuine laugh. "Oh, so chic. Some girls get diamonds. Some girls get semi-precious stones. Heck, some girls get rhinestones. Me? I get…" She tugged the out the contents, letting it all dangle from her fingers: a nail on a silver necklace chain.

"I'm not sure I get the message in this. You haven't gone psycho on me, have you? What's next? A box with an impaled pig's heart in it?"

Rob bit his bottom lip to try to hide his smile. This—Geena's humor, her smarts, the constant hard time she gave him—had endeared her to him faster than anything.

"Wait. Is this concrete?" she asked, running her fingers

down the nail.

"Yep," he said, too proud to come off as cool as he'd intended.

"This is *the* nail?"

He nodded. Three summers ago, Rob and Geena had emerged from The Page Turner bookstore to find a stretch of freshly poured sidewalk across the street. With Geena's hand in his, inspiration had overtaken him completely. He'd patted his pockets, scanned the ground, looking for anything that might work—a rock, a dropped quarter, even. His search carried him to the diner, a building that was undergoing a kind of once-in-twenty-year facelift, getting a whole new facade, emerging, finally, from the '70s. He'd found it under the scaffolding: a cluster of dropped nails. Rob had snatched one up and attacked the sidewalk square on the corner, carving his message into the wet cement. An out-in-the-open public promise to the girl he'd inexplicably found himself with every single Saturday night: *Rob & Geena 4Ever 1987.*

And now, here, he was giving her the nail that had carved the message, still surrounded by a few clumps of cement, because he hadn't wiped it off that well. Just kind of rubbed it off on the curb, then shoved it in the pocket of his jeans before grabbing Geena's hand again and running, both of them laughing the whole way.

He wanted her to remember it when she went off to college. Not just the sidewalk, but his promise, too (*4Ever*) and the fact that before her, he'd been the kid with too-long hair that most people had chalked up to being something of a rebel. *Trouble.* That was the word that had trailed him. He wanted Geena to remember that as the daughter of a cop, she had once seen him as a way to test her boundaries. He'd been the dip in the stomach that came when rounding the top curve of a roller-coaster or taking country roads twenty miles above the speed limit. He'd been the *this is probably going to all turn out fine but there's still a sliver of a chance it won't* thrill of danger.

In the beginning, he'd been something to play with, then escape from in the nick of time. He wasn't stupid. He knew that.

But there'd been more to it, later on—and *that* was what he wanted her to take with her to college in the fall. He wanted her to remember everything he'd done to prove himself worthy to her father. He wanted her to remember that when he'd severed himself from his silly, stereotypical bad boy reputation, she'd stayed.

Commencement was five months away. Still, though, it was hard to relax and enjoy the time he knew for sure they had left—the last semester of high school. He couldn't, because he didn't know how much time would follow graduation, if any.

He reached up to tuck her hair behind her ear. He did that often—it was his kiss on the cheek, his squeeze of the hand, his way to tell her his heart was overflowing.

"That's not going to be us, you know," Geena said, pointing to the radio, still playing "I Remember You." She finished working the clasp behind her neck, letting the nail dangle over her red sweatshirt.

"There's no need to have to remember something that hasn't ended. Something that will never end," she told him. "Right?"

Rob smiled. He knew, at that moment, she meant it. Just another thing to love about her. But even as he listened to her promise, he was infected with uncertainty.

5.

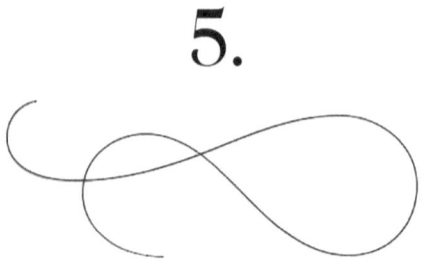

2018

TOM'S heart played a round of hopscotch as he stared at the words engraved into the sidewalk:

Rob & Geena 4Ever 1987

Thirty years ago, he'd regarded the message as a tattoo, more than he'd considered it graffiti. Rob and Geena, two naïve kids in their first-time-around love, a living, breathing "Jack and Diane," heartland teenagers and all that. Back then, tattoos had yet to become fashionable. Nobody had them, not really; they certainly didn't in Sullivan. Tattoos were for Hell's Angels or sailors or foolish, heartsick men too drunk to know better.

Tom had first gone to the corner to check out the message for himself after being teased about it by a coworker. There it was, exactly as it had been described to him: two names, a ridiculous declaration carved into the cement while it was still wet. If Tom had gotten there earlier, he would have used anything—a trowel purchased hurriedly from the nearby hardware store or the sole of his shoe or even his own hand—to smooth it out, erase what had been engraved.

But he was too late. The cement had hardened. All he could do was sigh sadly at the horrifically public mistake. One day, he knew, those two kids would regret their proclamation, irreversibly scrawled into what had then still been the busiest street in town, the same way any poor drunk fool would sober up, come to his senses, and regret the woman's name he'd had inked into his arm.

It was so juvenile to inscribe something so permanent—and visible—over some young love affair that was most likely never going to last.

Today, looking directly at the sidewalk square for the first time in ages, his chest constricted. He regretted it for the two kids all over again.

"First love, I bet," the construction worker remarked between swigs of coffee, his words laced with a somewhat sarcastic tone.

"Wonder where they got to," he went on. He finally put his bucket down—beside the sidewalk square rather than on it—and pulled a sandwich from a crumpled brown bag, his eyes still zeroed in on the words: *Rob & Geena 4Ever 1987.*

It made Tom a little uncomfortable, the intense way the stranger stared at the names. He wasn't sure what the man was picturing, but Tom knew firsthand love never stayed the same, no matter what your age. Love was constantly in motion, growing and shifting. Either it built up its muscles, or tragedy shot a lightning bolt into the space between you and the person you were closer to than anyone else on the planet, or the simple desire to stick your toes into that thick, lush grass on the opposite side of the fence got a little too strong. The ache of the unknown could be more destructive than dynamite.

First-timers like Rob and Geena never believed that, though. Everything with a sixteen-year-old occurred in terms of absolutes: I will *always* feel this way, I will *never* change my mind. I'll never get old, I'll always be young. The world has churned through a billion centuries to get to this point, and now, it can stop right here. This is it, that's that, end of story.

They had no idea that the world was constantly changing. That *they* were already changing. The very first time Tom had seen what those two kids had done to the sidewalk, he'd told himself that one day, half a blink away, they would be forty and the world would look nothing like it had when they were sixteen. Right on schedule, they would lean into their bathroom mirrors, counting their gray hairs while brushing their teeth, and they would say to themselves, "Huh. Wonder how that happened."

And after all those changes, the words on the sidewalk square would still exist.

Slowly, he became aware that Angela and the construction worker were playing a round of "What-If" with the two names.

"You know, there is a chance they might still be together," the hard hat suggested.

"Please," Angela muttered. "First love isn't exactly shelf-stable. Tends to spoil if you leave it out in the sun too long. And kids *always* wind up leaving it in the sun too long."

"Maybe they weren't kids."

"You think a couple of fifty-year-olds were out here carving their names? Is cement the traditional gift for the twenty-fifth anniversary?"

Tom couldn't stand it. He couldn't let them talk that way—not about Rob and Geena. It wasn't funny; it was making him angry enough to feel lightheaded, actually. Surely, that was the reason for the lightheadedness.

He needed to shut down their speculation, their storytelling. Rob and Geena were real people. Why were they talking about them like they were made up? "Rob's across the street," he blurted. His chest was burning. Why was this bothering him so much? He needed to chew a Rolaid.

Angela tossed her head back and laughed. Tom frowned. What did she think, that he was playing their game? That he was using this opportunity to tell some wild tale, get that giggle out of her? He wasn't. He was serious.

He touched his forehead. It was too cold to be sweating this much. And why did his coat suddenly feel so hot? Thirty-five degrees, the radio weatherman had announced as he'd pulled himself from his car twenty minutes ago.

"Tom?" Angela asked, her smile fading.

"Rob," Tom repeated, pointing at the sidewalk. "He owns the, ah—" He pointed toward The Page Turner. "I was just there. I was getting some…"

He didn't feel good. Why? Because he'd seen the sidewalk? Why would that make him feel this bad? Hadn't he made peace with that dumb old square long ago? Some childish destruction of public property. Those kids who had done it didn't exist anymore. Two adults had taken their place. When he thought of Rob and Geena, he thought of them in the present tense.

It had to be more than the sidewalk. This didn't feel like the intrusion of an old memory. He wasn't being protective. Something was wrong with him physically. Maybe he had the flu. Hadn't it been going around? He felt so strange.

"What about Geena?" the contractor asked, biting into a sardine sandwich, oblivious to the way Tom was sweating and trying harder to breathe. His own inhales sounded raspy inside his head.

He was swaying, too, wasn't he? Either that, or the sidewalk was suddenly unstable—it had waves, and he was a buoy, bobbing up and down.

"She's—she's my—daughter," Tom admitted. His voice rubbed, words like grains of sand in his throat.

"Your daughter?" the contractor repeated.

"That's *your* Geena?" Angela pressed.

"I…" Tom couldn't continue this conversation. His chest hurt. His jaw hurt. His arms hurt. Air was thick. He couldn't breathe.

He staggered forward. But his car was parked so far away. Two whole blocks. It hadn't seemed far when he'd arrived, but now—it might as well have been parked on the moon.

His knees buckled. *Throw your hands out*, he told himself. But his brain was all mushy and confused. He snorted a laugh at himself. Throw his hands out. Sure. There was no need to be afraid of falling. *The sidewalk isn't even hard anymore, remember?* he scolded himself. He had become a buoy, riding on the waves. Bobbing, bouncing along with the current.

He let go. Everything would be fine. He would crash

into the water and he would float back to his Geena, his daughter, who was supposed to be coming for Christmas.

Right before the world went black, he began to chant. "Geena, Geena, Geena…"

6.

ONE WEEK LATER

ROB called his son for what had to be the four thousandth time that afternoon as he fell into the back of the checkout line at The Red Apple, Sullivan's premiere (ahem, only) supermarket.

"You can't hide from me forever, you know," Rob warned. Cell phones still felt strange to him. Especially the voicemail thing. Like he was talking to himself in an empty house. Or worse yet, like he'd become Old Man Pinkering, the neighbor of his youth. The awful one who'd put bicycle-tire-popping spikes in his driveway to discourage kids from making U-turns and ran a non-stop grumbling commentary to himself on the State of the World—mostly, the high cost of everything and the rotten kids of the day, disrespectful down to their toenails.

"I know for a fact tomorrow's a teacher workday," he said, and paused, hoping Justin would finally pick up. *Could you still pick up after a call had gone to voicemail?* He was so horribly inept with these things. Thankfully, a bookstore owner didn't have to be a tech expert.

Rob sighed. "Look, come by the store, okay?" He closed by teasing, "Be good to see your ugly mug" in a transparent attempt to act nonchalant about the whole thing, like he'd also be cool with just seeing him again on his usual visitation day.

Rob suspected his son had a girlfriend, but Justin had been remarkably close-lipped about it. His mother certainly wouldn't tell Rob if he did. She and Rob hadn't exchanged more than two sentences in the past year. Like the last year of their marriage, déjà vu all over again.

A girlfriend, though—this, too, sent Rob off-kilter. Even more so than voicemail. Mostly because he felt so far removed from his own teenage years. When he tried to picture himself as he was back then, he saw Justin's face instead of his own. Youth felt to Rob like it happened to someone else.

He dropped his phone into his back pocket. If things with Maria were like they were ten years ago, he could have called her up and said, "Hey, how about figuring out how to send that kid of ours my way tomorrow, eh?" And she would have laughed and said something like, "Only if you feed him something decent. Orange jelly beans, contrary to popular opinion, are not actually made from oranges."

But then again, if things were like they were ten years ago, they would not be divorced, and they wouldn't be sharing their son.

Such a strange thing to share. Trading him back and forth. He wasn't a vacation home or a bicycle or a remote control, for God's sake.

And yet, here they were.

He stared at the headlines on the gossip rags. Better than to stare at the dinner he'd picked up—cup of tomato soup, garlic bread, and a side of iceberg lettuce with bacon bits from the salad bar, all tucked away nicely into one of those Styrofoam containers with the flip lid. The mandatory plastic fork. Single guy meal for one.

Depressing.

He could have asked Kelly, his one and only employee, if she wanted to grab dinner after work. But then again, Kelly had already skittered halfway out the door before he could finish turning the "Closed" sign toward the street. Anxious to get back to her own life.

The two women in front of him kept chatting away,

patting the curled ends of their short hair—one a chestnut brown and the other a Lucille Ball red. They laughed and they clucked and they tossed their gossip headlines back and forth.

Rob fought to keep from rolling his eyes. It was all so old-fashioned. Or maybe, in towns as small as Sullivan, gossip was simply timeless. A classic pastime that would never go out of style. Rob only half listened until he heard, in-between the beeps of the barcode scanner, "Tom Barrister had a heart attack."

Beep. Beep.

He gasped, his eyes widening. So that was why Tom hadn't been by the store. He usually stopped in at least twice a week. He devoured Westerns. In paperback.

"How terrible! Is he okay?"

"On the road to a full recovery."

Rob sighed with relief.

"Oh. Whew. That's good. That's good."

Beep. Beep.

Rob pulled out his phone. He needed to call Tom. He surely wasn't answering, but Rob would endure the voicemail thing for him—especially now. He'd ask if he needed anything. Someone else had to be helping him out, checking his messages. Maybe Mrs. Cranston. After all, she'd lived next door to the Baristers for years.

Rob was halfway through dialing the number when one of the women commented, "Yes, and you know, I heard his daughter's back home. While he recuperates. Nurse him back to his rascally old self."

Beep.

Rob froze, his finger hovering a few centimeters over his phone.

"Isn't she still teaching at the university? Iowa, isn't it?"

Beep.

"Oh, yes. Got someone else to take over her classes. Semester's about over. She can grade the finals herself, you know. Have her students email their tests to her. So dedicated, that one."

"Yes, and such a nice daughter, that Geena."

"Yes. Have you tried those new Cinnamon Frosted Flakes yet?"

Beep, beep, beep.

Now Rob didn't know what he wanted to do. Yes, Tom was one of his best customers. Yes, they had a long history between them. Yes, Rob had grown to honestly like the man. But if Geena was home, that complicated matters. After high school, their lives had taken separate paths.

Looking back, it seemed to have happened almost immediately after graduation. Shortly after his stint in the service,

Geena was already so long-gone that Rob found himself married to someone else. He and his wife had bounced around, state to state, each of them snatching up one unsatisfactory job after another. Along the way, they'd had their son.

On little more than a whim and a phone call from his mother in which she'd announced his favorite store, The Page Turner, was for sale ("and you know, that nice Scott Drummond at the bank is *so anxious* to get someone into it—an old Sullivanite like yourself with plenty of local references still in town would have such a great shot at a loan"), Rob had brought his family home.

In the divorce, he'd been willing to give up everything else—the house, both cars—as long as he got the store. He'd have slept in the store if he had to. Maria had snickered in victory as she'd signed the papers, agreeing to their settlement, their who-got-what. Yes, the bookstore was struggling. Most businesses in Sullivan were struggling. But Rob still believed in love. All kinds and shades of love. And he loved that old store. The same way he'd loved it when he was younger and had practically lived in the Sci-Fi aisles.

Still, though. Did he call? If he did, Geena would maybe answer.

Rob dropped his phone back into his pocket. Geena knew where to find him, surely. She regularly visited her dad.

Tom always had new little anecdotes to share, tales of his visiting daughter, the professor. Almost like he intended to keep Rob up-to-date on her life. He'd often wondered if the stories he told Tom got passed to Geena when he returned home.

Funny, though—Tom had never come to the store when she was in town. And Geena had certainly never visited herself. Not once in the years he'd owned The Page Turner.

What did that mean he should do now? She was upset. Her father'd had a heart attack. She surely wouldn't want to see him at this point. Wouldn't want to add an awful, awkward encounter to her worried, frenzied, overfull plate. Would she?

Then again, by now, weren't they past all that stuff? Hadn't the water finally calmed down under that bridge? Could he bring by a casserole and assure her if she needed anything, she could call—and he wouldn't ever let it go to that crummy old voicemail?

Wasn't there a point in your life when you could just be friends?

He finally realized the checker was shouting at him, "PLASTIC OKAY?" in that annoyed way that implied she'd been trying to get him to answer the same question for the last ten minutes or so as she clicked her watermelon-scented gum and pointed at the stack of bags at the edge of the checkout counter.

He nodded limply. "Fine," he answered.

He stumbled through paying. But instead of driving home, he drove back to the bookstore. Maybe he was hoping the gossipers were headed that way. Maybe he felt like he needed a little more information—another juicy tidbit or twelve—before deciding whether or not to go out to Tom's place.

He didn't find a gossiper, though. Instead, he found Angela.

7.

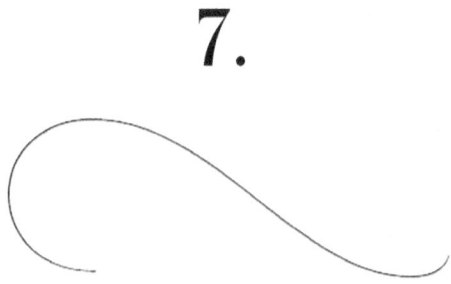

"FORGET something?" Angela called out.

Rob stopped, his sneakers dragging against the sidewalk. He looked somewhat bewildered and a little sad, like something unspeakable had happened to him. Everything about him suddenly had the appearance of having been tortured—the wrinkled front of his button-down shirt, the heavy military surplus pea coat hanging at a strange angle and flapping open in the wind, the roughed-up bill of his Royals cap, the fraying laces on his dirty Converse sneakers.

"Lose something?" Angela corrected herself. Judging by his expression, he'd discovered something he'd always depended on was gone forever.

Rob shook his head. "No, I—" He lifted the cap to scratch the side of his head, exposing his gray-streaked hair in the process. The plastic grocery bag in his other hand rustled. "Did you know Tom Barister had a heart attack?"

"I knew." Angela shoved the rim of her own brown hat a little higher on her forehead—almost as though this would help her see Rob better. "I was there when Tom had his heart attack. Right on this sidewalk, actually."

"It happened out here? How could I have missed it? I never heard sirens," Rob protested.

"There weren't any. Turned out, I had a contractor who'd been to one of those NASCAR driving schools. He swore he'd be faster than any ambulance. He was, too."

Rob looked wan and sickly.

"He's going to be okay, you know," Angela offered. "Tom, I mean. A minor heart attack, that was what the doctor said. And he's got plenty of help. In fact, his daughter—"

Her eyes instantly zipped down to the sidewalk square: *Rob & Geena 4Ever.*

Should she mention Geena was home? Should she not? Had she already said too much?

"I'm not sure what I'm doing out here," Rob confessed. "I was on my way home. Just stopped to get dinner. But then I overheard what happened to Tom, and I got so—"

"—flummoxed," Angela finished. For some reason, her grandmother's old phrases were finding her often lately.

"Yeah," Rob agreed. He glanced down at his sack. "I'm sorry—you have things to do. I should go eat my dinner and…"

"No way," Angela announced. "You're coming inside with me. You look like a man who could use a drink." *And someone to talk to*, she could have added, but didn't.

"Do you actually have something to drink in there?" he asked around a crooked grin.

She held the door open. "Come on. I'll show you around."

Rob finally nodded a reluctant and not-too-convinced *all right*.

"I wish I could say you're the first person to get the grand tour, but I have given one other person a glance or two," Angela admitted, happily ushering him inside, where the perfume of sawdust and fresh paint filled their noses. "We're putting it all back exactly the way it was. I was lucky. Most of the original furnishings—all the tables and chairs—were still here. None of the other would-be buyers who thought about reopening got far enough to throw them out. And once I got the mold off, shined everything up with a little wood polish, everything looked good as new. Better, really. Nobody makes furniture like this now. And the *bar*—" She pointed toward it with pride. "This thing would cost a fortune if you tried to make a custom piece like that now. It's so big. Like somehow it was created right here, carved inside this room, so that it could never be removed. I—"

Rob's expression was not exactly registering enthusiasm. Quite the opposite, in fact, as he took in the propped-open ladders and the spread-open tarps and the buckets of construction adhesive and the wires hanging down from the ceiling.

"Doesn't your sign out front say you're opening on Christmas Eve?" he asked.

Angela shrugged, but his words still punched her right in the gut. "We've hit a few snags. Nothing that's going to knock us off course."

Rob nodded in an *if you say so* kind of gesture. "I was only in here once before," he admitted. "But Ruby had already died, if I remember right. And the place was looking kind of shabby."

"Oh, that's too bad," Angela moaned. "You really missed out on something special."

8.

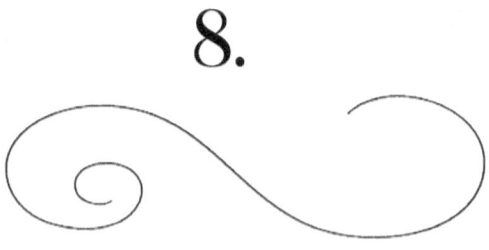

1979

ANGELA didn't run or skip into Ruby's. At fourteen years old, she had left skipping behind.

But that was fine—exciting, actually. Sure, even when Angela had been a skipper, in her Mary Janes and tights, she had been pretty. That's what little girls were. They were pretty. Women—they were beautiful, a word that didn't just describe their looks but also indicated they had snared a bit of power. *Pretty* girls were admired briefly, smiled at. But a *beautiful* woman could potentially bend men to her will. Angela was becoming beautiful. Which meant the world was about to belong to her.

She walked, head held high, side-by-side with Aunt Elizabeth, down the street toward Ruby's Place, the premiere spot for special nights out. For celebrations. The place to wear your best clothes and the jewelry handed down for three generations. To feel, for an evening, like something of a celebrity. To feel welcome and adored—no matter what your age. Kids from one to ninety-two, as the old carol promised.

As a girl, Angela had looked to Elizabeth—a woman who rivaled movie stars in her own appearance—for a kind of wordless instruction on how to package beauty. How to dress it up, how to adorn it, what color lipstick it should wear. Angela wasn't the only one, of course. Elizabeth owned the most successful women's dress shop in town. She'd styled every female within a hundred miles of Sullivan, dressing them for every important event in their lives. Why, she'd even styled Ruby herself, the current owner of the pub where Elizabeth and Angela were about to spend their Christmas celebration for two.

Yes, Angela had long considered Elizabeth's earrings and updo to be the crowning symbols of womanhood. She had often told herself that once she was able to wear them both and not look like a kid in a ridiculous Halloween costume, she would have officially arrived. She would be nothing short of a woman herself.

This year, in addition to the silver three-inch heels and the long black wool dress coat Elizabeth had gifted to Angela from the shop, her hair had been pinned to the top of her head and a pair of large silver wreath earrings had been clipped to her lobes.

She was pleased to see, as she and Elizabeth passed Ruby's front window, that her reflection proved she did not look foolish. Just the opposite. She looked lovely.

She had arrived.

Beautiful. People were going to begin using that word to describe her. In fact, if she listened, she might hear it a few times that very night.

Inside the pub, she peeled her coat off to expose her winter white crepe gown—complete with long sleeves, a mock turtleneck, a flowing, ankle-length skirt, and a winter white leather belt with a silver buckle. Her silver clutch had been fastened with a large red glass poinsettia brooch. Elizabeth had recognized that the time had come for Angela to opt for only classy, womanly expressions of holiday cheer. No junky plastic jewelry, no jingle bell ankle bracelets, no felt Santa hats.

Scott Drummond was already seated at a table with his father, Walter, the current manager of the bank. He was looking a bit out of place, though. Awkward. Angela was still straightening her belt when she noticed him. It was a strange thing to be around Scott when she was not looking like her usual self, the schoolgirl in a ponytail and penny loafers. They had been classmates since the beginning of time, had known each other since the days of sandboxes and coloring books. Scott was in a suit and tie nearly identical to his dad's. Come to think of it, it was strange to be around Scott when he was not looking like his usual self, either—a schoolboy in jeans and one of his white baseball shirts with the colored sleeves.

Angela narrowed her eyes at Scott, but not to glare. She wanted to blur her eyes so that she could picture Scott sitting at a desk at the bank, like his dad. Elizabeth had taken her there a few times to deposit the daily earnings from her store. Walter had a picture of Scott on the corner of his desk, right behind his basket of suckers.

Officially, Angela thought with not even the faintest whiff of sadness, she was through with suckers.

She sashayed across the room, making sure to remember to stand up straight. Aunt Elizabeth had often reminded her that her height of five-foot-ten was something to be proud of.

She took a stool for herself, aware she was the youngest customer by far at the bar. She immediately hiked the hem of her dress up over her ankle so that everyone could see she was wearing heels and expensive silk stockings.

"Hot chocolate, extra plate of marshmallows," Ruby said, smiling at her in a way that said she was proud to have remembered Angela's usual.

52

Angela hesitated. It was such a kid thing to order.

Ruby was right, though. Angela and Elizabeth had been having girls-night-out Christmas celebrations at the classy supper club for years. It was, in fact, their special time together, with fancy silverware and linen tablecloths. Always, they wore new dresses. In their very earliest visits, Angela had worn pigtails on each side of her head, secured with red velvet ribbon.

This year was supposed to be different. This was the first year she had come as a woman.

And yet, she really wanted those marshmallows.

Ruby leaned forward. "How about we get Elizabeth to deviate from her usual champagne and join in for the hot chocolate?" she suggested with a wink. She was looking especially lovely, her hair a bright silver—not gray—festive, like the tinsel that draped the mirror.

Angela grinned, turning toward the stool beside her to raise her eyebrows, wordlessly asking if Elizabeth would do just that.

But Elizabeth wasn't there. Someone else—a man— was pulling the stool back, pointing his date toward it.

"Wait," Angela barked. "That's for my—"

But where was she? Where had Elizabeth gone?

Angela frowned, twisting around. It was hard to see in the candlelight, with so many bodies coming and going.

It wasn't as though she could shout, either. Elizabeth would never hear her own name. Not with the piano pounding out "Hark, the Herald Angels Sing" and so many voices belting out a new verse in unison. Couples danced, spinning each other. Laughter burst as boughs of mistletoe were tugged from pockets and dangled over heads. Children on their best behavior squealed when they saw their best friends and offered, in their high-pitched voices, to share their candy canes, snapping them off at the neck. One table surrounded by revelers exchanging brightly wrapped gifts erupted in rounds of *oooh*s and *ahhhh*s each time a surprise was pulled from a box.

There she was. By the entrance. Elizabeth. Still in her winter white cashmere overcoat. Before Angela had a chance to sigh with relief, she realized Elizabeth had one hand pressed on the door, the other balled into a fist in front of her mouth.

She was coughing. Angela could tell, even though she couldn't hear her over the din. Coughing hard—face growing increasingly redder, like she couldn't stop.

Elizabeth lowered her fist and straightened, her chest swelling with a visibly deep breath.

She wiped her forehead. And took a moment to gather herself.

When she caught Angela staring, she threw her own shoulders back and hurried toward the bar.

It hit Angela for the first time that Elizabeth was also getting older. But she quickly brushed it off. It couldn't be anything serious. Of course not. Surely, it was nothing more than a mild winter cold.

"Two hot chocolates?" Angela croaked as Elizabeth slipped out of her coat.

"Fine, fine," Elizabeth said, propping herself on her stool.

"I have a peppermint," Angela offered, hoping it would soothe her aunt's dry winter throat.

Elizabeth smiled and slipped the peppermint from her hand.

"How you doing, kid?" Ruby asked, sliding two hot chocolates onto the bar, along with two plates of marshmallows. Angela swallowed a giggle. She knew that the "kid" part wasn't directed toward her. It was Ruby's nickname for Elizabeth.

Elizabeth shot Angela a warning look as she reached for the marshmallows. Homemade and toasted and very hot. Angela took a bite. As usual, she was too eager and the bite was too big. It burned her mouth.

Still trying to breathe through her mouth to cool it all off, Angela expected Elizabeth to give her a *Do you have to do that every year?* kind of look.

Only, Elizabeth had already turned her attention elsewhere, staring off in the distance.

Ruby nodded, as though seeming to translate the volumes of meaning in Elizabeth's sigh.

"Got somebody after you, kid?"

Elizabeth grinned. So did Angela. The two women had been a kind of gang of two the last several years. They'd become businesswomen in their "second act"s, as Elizabeth was always phrasing it. *Late in life*, others called it.

They understood each other as no one else did. They commiserated on the occasional disappointing sales report. They dealt each other advice on how not to be taken advantage of by men who still believed a nice dose of sabotage might send a self-proclaimed businesswoman back to the kitchen where she belonged.

"So many changes," Elizabeth said wistfully, as if talking more to herself than to Ruby.

"Business at the dress shop slowing?" Ruby asked.

"No. The opposite. It's as busy as ever. Maybe busier. Hard for an old woman to keep up with it all," she said, nudging Angela playfully.

Angela didn't think it was funny, especially after that coughing business. She didn't like the idea of Elizabeth referring to herself as an old woman.

"Oh, don't worry about her," Ruby moaned, seeing that her aunt's response had bothered Angela. "She's fishing for a compliment about how young and gorgeous she looks tonight. Pretending she's sick. Yeah, right."

Elizabeth rolled her eyes. "I do have a cold," she muttered. "A *cold*," she repeated, scolding Ruby.

It was Ruby's turn to roll her eyes.

Elizabeth and Ruby chattered on, telling each other inside jokes. At least, that was what Angela told herself when the two women laughed as Ruby teased Elizabeth for standing out in the snow "kissing Santa Claus"—clearly a euphemism, one whose meaning they intended to keep between each other.

The longer it went on, though, the less Angela understood. And it was not all private jokes and hidden meaning. The two weren't speaking in code. It was straightforward—the conversation of two women telling stories of their days, their customers, their lives. With each new sentence, Angela felt herself shrinking. Because she realized that a real woman—one who had, in fact, truly arrived—would have known what it all meant.

Angela had piled her hair onto the top of her head prematurely. She was as out of place in her heels and earrings as poor Scott was in his suit. Glancing behind her shoulder, she caught him trying to wedge a finger between his neck and his

Windsor knot.

She tugged her clip earrings off her lobes and dropped them into her purse. As Elizabeth and Ruby's conversation grew increasingly more animated, Angela slipped her feet out of her shoes. Giving Scott a shrug, she padded across the floor, disappearing into the crowd surrounding the piano.

After all, Ruby's wasn't a place to mourn or feel embarrassed—at least, not for long. So what if she wasn't quite there yet? So what if *beautiful* and *womanly* were words still a few years away? She was here, and it was the holiday season, and the whole place felt as merry as the inside of a Christmas tree.

And that, quite frankly, was pretty wonderful, too.

9.

2018

FUNNY—some details of the very last Christmas Eve she'd ever spent with Elizabeth were as clear to Angela as anything that had happened last week. And others were so utterly fuzzy, she questioned whether they were real or details she'd made up to fill in the blanks.

But it always happened that way, she supposed. At least, it did when the last times sneaked up on you. When you knew for sure you were in the midst of something final—when you were breaking up with someone or graduating or leaving one job for another—you could tell yourself, "I'll never climb these stairs again," or "I'll never kiss him again," and you could make a conscious effort to memorize every detail.

Of course, even then, it never worked completely. Time

59

could still blur the details you'd made a point to preserve. But the fading happened quicker with the events you didn't know were the last. Those memories were the first to go.

One thing remained certain regarding that Christmas Eve of 1979: Angela's realization that there were so many things she did not know was the very first adult thought she'd ever had.

The idea made her chuckle softly.

"What?" Rob asked.

"Nothing, I—what'd you get for dinner?" Angela asked, eager to change the subject.

"Soup and salad."

"Well, feel free to spread out on the bar. Got some great beers in the other day."

As she pointed to the stools, Angela caught a glimpse of her reflection in the mirror behind where the top shelf bottles would eventually be displayed. Such a different reflection than she'd found that Christmas Eve back in 1979.

She'd been led astray by the idea that youthful beauty would make her life easy. It hadn't. Of course not. The worst part being that everyone assumed a beautiful woman already had love and open doors. Nothing could have been further from the truth. After failures and lost love and an extensive collection of disappointments, this bar was perhaps her last chance for something exciting. Something important.

She brushed her thoughts aside and disappeared into the kitchen. She made a beeline for the industrial cooler, which the electrician had told her roughly fifty-three times should not have been working. He was right—it *should* have died long ago.

Angela had a pretty good idea what (or, rather, who) was making it hum, and it had become one of her daily chores to keep him from looking into the cooler too intently. Magic, she'd told herself, shouldn't have been weak enough to be derailed by a couple of newly-spliced wires, but then again, who knew? Maybe magic, like electricity, could suffer power surges and shortages. Maybe, if he mucked around too much, he could blow magic's fuse, and every last one of Angela's plans could go up in smoke.

Best to make sure the electrician had too many other jobs to do to bother with that old cooler.

Angela reached inside, grabbed two bottles by the neck, and headed back into the belly of the bar.

"You have to try this spiced ale," Angela announced, plunking the bottles down—one for her and one for Rob. She flicked the caps off, adding, "Not sure it'll make you want to give up eggnog, exactly, but it's quickly become one of my favorites."

She took a swig, watching over the brown edge of the bottle as Rob followed suit. He had placed his pea coat and his ball cap on the bar. His cheeks and the tips of his ears were bright pink from the cold, and his eyes still looked as though he was trying to figure something out.

Angela wanted to help him—although her newfound desire wasn't exactly selfless. She'd spent the past year planning to be the bartender for Ruby's. That was how the whole thing was going to work: she'd talk her customers up, find out who was open to seeing everything the bar had to offer. She'd find out who had a hole in their heart. A hole that the bar had the power to mend.

And then?

Well, that's when the magic would kick in.

In the meantime, Rob was offering Angela the perfect bartending practice run. Time to start coaxing secrets out.

"Tom is the other person I let inside," she said, hoping to use it as a springboard for conversation. "He was awfully interested in what I had going on over here. Kept asking and asking—he'd stop by every time he came to your shop for a new book. Finally, I let him take a peek."

Rob nodded, digging his thumbnail under the label on his bottle.

But it didn't prod him into adding anything.

Angela's head spun. "Tom told me about the sidewalk," she blurted. "The part of it that has your name carved into it. We were talking about it right before he had his heart attack."

"You were?" Rob's face twisted into a new expression, though Angela wasn't quite sure of what. Guilt, maybe. Like she had implied that simply remembering his and Geena's cement-scribbling could have somehow triggered a myocardial infarction.

"I must've walked down that sidewalk ten thousand times, and I never would have thought that Rob was you." Angela leaned forward, dropping her elbows onto the bar, lowering her voice in a manner that implied whatever was said would remain forever between the two of them. "I had an engagement that ended so poorly. I still feel bad about it. It's just one of those things—I mean, even if you don't regret the fact that something ended, you can still regret how messy it got at the end."

Rob shook his head. "That wasn't how it went at all. Not me and Geena. It was never bad. Or messy. We never had a fight. After high school, she went to college and I went to the service."

He shrugged. "Everybody's got a story like that, don't they? It's so strange how there can be this person in your life— the *most* important person in your life—and you just…drift apart. We kept in touch for a little while, writing back and forth, and we always tried to meet up here in town, but it wasn't like we were both in school and had the same schedule. Anytime I was here, she was gone, and vice versa. It was like we were totally out of sync.

"And then, the letters got farther between and—I dunno, it's like you get to a point that if you haven't heard from someone for several months, you figure they probably want it that way. She moved on. Found a nice college guy, I'm sure." He raised his bottle and took a distracted swig.

"You almost say that like you were opposites," Angela argued. "The book girl and the guy in the service. You're a book guy. Obviously." She nodded in the direction of The Page Turner.

"Ah, yeah, I know," Rob conceded, waving his free hand. "I was always into it—reading, I mean—but I wasn't the kind to write a bunch of stuffy papers in school. Sometimes, you have a feeling for something, and when you start to pick it apart too much, it vanishes. If that makes sense." He took another swig before divulging, "We used to have reading dates. Me and Geena. Can you believe it? We'd find a secluded place and we'd park, and instead of making out, we'd sit together and read, me some sci-fi thing and her some Jane Austen Mr. Darcy thing."

"Can't say I've ever done that," Angela observed.

Rob let out a long, audible sigh—the kind of noise people make seeing a new baby or a work of art for the first time. "When it's with somebody you're really close to, it's practically spiritual." He raised his bottle again, shrugged, added, "Of course, making out isn't bad, either."

Angela laughed and stopped Rob before he had a chance to pick up his plastic spoon. His dinner was nothing more than a sad handful of iceberg lettuce that had started to brown in some sections and watery soup that looked like the canned variety. She couldn't let him eat that.

"I have a few supplies in the kitchen—other than the liquor, I mean. Would you mind if I kind of livened up this— *thing*—whatever it is?" she asked, gesturing toward his Styrofoam container.

"Please," Rob said, holding his hands up and leaning away, showing her that he had no intention of fighting her on the matter.

Angela raced back into the kitchen, where she instantly started to pace. "Think," she muttered under her breath. "Think."

She was something of a stranger to the world of whisks and cutlery knives, having mostly relied on take-out herself. She had a couple of cooks lined up for her grand opening, but she was the only one who knew Ruby's signature recipes—and she'd been sworn to secrecy. She needed to be at least semi-capable both behind the bar and in the kitchen. Again, Rob was offering her a practice run.

"Come on, come on, girl," she chanted. "You can do this."

Only, she didn't exactly have the pantry fully stocked—not yet. Mostly odds and ends. Primarily, she'd begun to order food with the idea that treating her renovators to a late afternoon snack would encourage them to work longer hours. Make the Christmas Eve deadline feel not quite so out of reach.

She tugged at the cooler door and various drawers and cabinets. In the end, she re-toasted Rob's two pieces of garlic bread, turning it into a roast beef sandwich, complete with Swiss cheese and horseradish mayonnaise. With the help of another can of undiluted Campbell's and a few herbs, she managed to transform the sad, watery tomato mess into a thick, rich tomato and basil soup.

She could only hope the flavors would meld together. She placed Rob's jazzed-up dinner on heavy white restaurant-quality dishes—the same dishes that had been in storage for the last few decades. She tossed the Styrofoam into the trash.

"Here we go," she announced, popping the swinging kitchen door open with her hip, and delivering his plate with an embellished turn of the wrist.

"Hey," Rob said, perking. "That sure smells better than what I started with." He took a giant bite of the sandwich and said, his words muffled, "It *is* better than what I had to begin with." And gave her a thumbs-up.

Angela beamed and wiped the top of the bar with a rag. She'd seen bartenders do that on TV.

Rob swallowed, paused for a moment, admitted, "I want to call on him—Tom, I mean—but I'm not sure I should." He cringed, made a face, held his hands out. "Call on him?" he repeated incredulously. "Where'd that come from? Talk about old-fashioned. I can't be that old." He shook his head at himself. "I need to start blasting my Metallica records as soon as I get home."

Angela laughed again as he lifted his sandwich for another bite.

"Why shouldn't you go? Is it because of Geena?" Angela asked.

Rob nodded. He worked his jaw back and forth, using his tongue to try to dislodge a piece of meat from a crevice between his teeth.

"She's going through something hard," he finally said, "and I'm probably the last person she wants to see. So what if it didn't necessarily end badly? It ended, and right now, she's got to have less than zero interest in drudging up the past."

He wiped his fingers on the paper napkin Angela'd brought and frowned, growing pensive.

"I didn't know Tom until recently," Angela said, hoping to keep the conversation rolling forward. "I mean, I knew who he was—everyone knew that, him being a police officer. But I'd never met him until I bought Ruby's Place. And as for you guys, or his ties to Geena, that was a surprise, too. I was in college in 1987. Missed the whole sidewalk carving thing."

"Man, he used to hate my guts," Rob said. He took another bite of sandwich, chewing thoughtfully. Finally, he continued, "It was different after I came back to town. Like you said—you're older and you get to know people differently. Tom would stop by to shop and tell me these long-winded stories about her. I know she's been in town, too, but she never came by, not once. Maybe the whole thing's embarrassing to her now. Maybe, if somebody were to ever point to that sidewalk out there, she'd shrug it off, say it was somebody else with the same name."

Angela couldn't help but smile at the way their conversation about Tom kept circling back to Geena.

He picked up the stainless steel spoon Angela had given him to replace the flimsy plastic one in cellophane. "The only thing I know for sure is that ever since I heard about Tom, I've been thinking about—all of it. About her and—what it was. To be sixteen. What it was like when life could still be anything. Because I hadn't really made any choices yet, you know? There were millions of options to choose from. More than a million. It was *limitless*. Everything was fresh and new and the only things in the world that had been around long enough to fade belonged to other people. Life smelled like a—" Rob stopped, shaking his head.

"Like a what?" Angela pressed.

"Like a sixteen-year-old girl. Not just any sixteen-year-old girl. The sixteen-year-old girl who was completely out of my league, but wanted to be with me, anyway." Rob raised his eyes sheepishly.

Angela put her hand on his arm. She hoped it felt warm and reassuring rather than strange and unwelcome.

He didn't pull away, at least. That had to be a good sign.

"I can't go out there," Rob announced. "Not to Tom's place. I'll wait till he comes back to the store."

Angela nodded as though agreeing—or at the very least, respecting his decision. Should she have, though? Had he spilled his guts to her hoping she'd encourage him to go?

He finished eating, wiped his mouth, and patted the bar a couple of times before hoisting himself from his stool.

Angela held up a finger. "Wait," she said, and raced

into the kitchen. She didn't figure Rob for a cocktail kind of person, so she put together a kind of sampler six-pack of the beers she'd ordered, lined them up in a small cardboard box.

"Merry Christmas," she announced, banging through the kitchen door and holding the box toward him.

"Oh, I couldn't. You already saved my supper," he said, gesturing toward his now-empty plate.

"It's Christmas, and I feel like giving you a present."

Rob smiled. "Well, I'll accept. But only if you let me find a way to give you something in return."

"How about being my door greeter?"

"Come again?"

"On Christmas Eve," she said. "I need a handsome door greeter. Someone to welcome customers, help them find a place to sit. People cluster by the door too long—tend to clog the space. Up for it?"

"I'd be honored." He raised the cardboard box. "Thanks for these. And I'll see you on Christmas Eve."

Angela smiled, walked him to the door. After it had fallen shut—after she'd watched Rob walk down the street, disappearing into the pitch black night—she glanced around her half-finished bar and sighed, "We can only hope."

10.

1995

HER bar was closed. The "Available for Lease" and "Out of Business" signs had been taped to the inside of the front window. For the first time in half a century, Ruby's Place was no longer serving the people of Sullivan on Christmas Eve.

Ruby sighed, standing in the middle of the empty establishment.

She was the only one left. She had been here, alone, for what had to have been months and months—hard to know for sure, since time for her had no boundaries. It offered no structure, no beginning or end. Time was impossible to keep track of after life was over.

Not that anyone would have suspected she was still around. Everyone walked by, seeing only a deserted space.

For them, Ruby was nothing more than a memory. But why wouldn't she be? After all, Ruby had already passed away a handful of Christmas Eves ago.

Ruby wasn't sure what to call herself. A ghost? A memory? None of it fit. She felt as real as she ever had.

After her death, a few members of her family had stepped in to keep the old bar going—a cousin, a half-sibling. But it wasn't the same.

"A bad imitation," Ruby's customers had repeatedly grumbled, rarely leaving a tip before hurrying back out the door. New customers couldn't even be coaxed inside with the promise of the cheapest beer in town. Ruby's was supposed to offer far more than a competitive price of beer on tap, more than bargain basement well drinks. Everybody was already in the habit of getting the cheap stuff from the roadhouse on the edge of town.

And so, with heavy hearts, the "Closed" sign had been turned toward the street for the last time.

It made Ruby feel good and horrible all at once. She liked knowing the place wasn't the same without her. But then again, her own bar—the place she had spent decades creating, building, and caring for—had become an antique, a relic from a bygone era, included only in the photo gallery at the small Sullivan History Museum.

Now, here she was, alone on Christmas Eve with no customers to serve. What was she to do with herself? To fill the empty minutes, she began to practice dancing, as she once had on the stage.

Ruby slipped nimbly between tables. "Who would have thought," she announced, "that the professional, world-traveled ballerina would have found a second career serving up whiskey sours in tiny Sullivan, Missouri?" She giggled to herself, remembering the scowls that had once been directed her way by Roy Weber, owner of the electronics store across the street. She'd loved parading in front of her shop while the old guy watched, puffing away on his cigarettes, a regular angry fire-breathing dragon.

She pirouetted around the edge of the bar—and gracefully raised her arms above her head to signal the end of her performance—to no orchestra and no applause. And no customers.

Ruby lowered her arms. She had let go of something she'd loved once. She'd let go of dance. She had succeeded in reinventing herself. But letting go of her bar had proven itself to be an unattainable goal. She mourned it differently. Maybe because the time to reinvent herself was over. She was a carved date on a headstone, a final line in a book. The curtain had fallen permanently.

But that didn't seem quite right, either. How could the curtain have fallen, how could the opportunity for reinvention be gone? She was still here.

Her current existence was lonely, though. And loneliness was the steepest rent she'd ever paid.

"You know why it seems lonely?" Ruby said out loud, hands on her hips. "Because it's Christmas Eve and the place isn't decorated!"

She raced into the storage room, hauling out cardboard boxes and tightly balled-up strings of lights. She propped the plastic "Merry Christmas!" sign on the bar. She tied sprigs of artificial pine to the sconces. She unfolded the small aluminum tree that had stood near the entrance for years. She draped tinsel around the mirror behind the top shelf bottles. She lit the candles in the center of every table. She put an old Bing Crosby holiday album on her record player and chose her favorite tune.

As the sounds of "White Christmas" filled the space, Ruby mixed herself a Long Island iced tea. She raised her glass, feeling the need to make a toast. "To—" Her smile faded. "To what?" she asked herself. "The new year? Times gone by? Christmas in my old spot?"

She exhaled deeply, her shoulders drooping. "Does it even matter?"

One thing was certain: a one-sided toast was about as

satisfying as clapping with one hand. Maybe, she thought, it would help if another cocktail was sitting on the bar. So what if it didn't technically belong to anyone? She could clink the lips of the glasses together and pretend that it somehow soothed that lonely ache inside of her.

She kept the second drink simple, pouring a scotch neat.

Suddenly, with no warning, the door to the kitchen flapped open.

Ruby skittered backward. Was someone coming to look the place over? Why? Had she misjudged the date? Was it not really Christmas Eve? Would they see her? Would they be frightened by the appearance of her holiday decorations, or think they were nothing more than a joke?

A man paused in the doorway, glancing about the bar. He looked strangely out of place in a wide olive tie and poly-ester shirt—as though he'd walked right out of the '70s. What was going *on*?

"Hey, Rubes," the man greeted. He pointed at the glass. "You remembered." He propped himself on the stool directly behind the drink.

"Of course I did…Walter. Walter Drummond!" she exclaimed as it started to come back to her. "From the bank." Yes, Walter, who had been one of her very most reliable customers through the Carter administration. Walter, who had died—what? A decade ago? Ruby couldn't be sure. Time was a landscape she could no longer navigate.

She clapped her hands. "Walter!"

He twisted his face in confusion. "You okay, Rubes?"

She laughed. "Yeah. It's just—I'm so glad to see you."

"You too," Walter agreed. He raised his glass. "Merry Christmas, Rubes!"

Ruby raised her own. "Merry Christmas," she agreed, and clinked her glass against his.

As she took a sip, an idea struck Ruby with the force of a sledgehammer. She grabbed the gin and vermouth, and speared three olives on a toothpick.

As if on command, the back Employees Only door flopped open. A woman entered in a bright red sequined jacket.

"Hey, Evie." Ruby waved at the same smiling face that had once greeted customers from the piano bench.

"Hey yourself, darlin'," Evie replied.

Ruby raced to her record player. She raised the needle and asked, "You don't mind playing for us, do you, Evie? I'd much rather listen to you."

"I always was the world's biggest sucker for compliments," Evie responded with a wink. She cradled the tapered end of the martini glass, carrying it toward the piano. She placed the glass on top of the old upright, sat on the bench, and began to play a few warm-up chords.

Ruby was so happy, she didn't even bark at Evie about using a coaster, as she once had. Oh, she'd once gotten after Evie, really blistered her with her tongue-lashings, every time she'd left a white ring on the piano.

"Hey!" Walter shouted. "Don't you dare play some sentimental schmaltzy thing, okay?"

He stood, carrying his own drink toward the piano, chattering as he walked, giving Evie a list of the carols he most wanted to hear.

Ruby was energized. And onto something. She grabbed a lime and a club soda, and mixed a gin rickey. Staring into it, she wondered, for the tiniest of moments, where the limes and the olives had come from.

Before she had time to get too concerned about it, a woman stepped out of the shadows of the old cloak room. She wore a slinky ivory colored gown.

"Dorothy," Ruby greeted the old jazz singer, the one who had still worn her cloche hats long after they were no longer popular.

The singer smiled beneath her hat, raising her glass to Ruby in another toast.

Ruby was off, mixing whiskey sours and rum and Cokes, racking her memory for the favorites of her regulars. With each drink, another face appeared. They were back. They were all back—plus some.

Even as she worked her muddler and her blender and her shaker, there was one drink—maybe the simplest of all—that she realized she was avoiding. Maybe because she was afraid it might not work. And if it didn't—well, that would be a disappointment she wasn't quite sure she could bear.

Finally, once the bar was full—once voices were shouting and singing and it felt as though literally everything in her life was coming back to hug her again—Ruby took a deep breath and grabbed a bottle of champagne.

She popped the cork and poured a glass.

And shut her eyes. Crossed her fingers.

Please please please please please, she began to chant silently.

Finally, hesitantly, Ruby cracked one eye to find a lovely female figure sitting at the stool behind the champagne glass—wearing a black velvet gown, large rhinestone pin on her left shoulder, red lipstick, blond updo.

"Hey, kid," Ruby sighed, smiling at her oldest friend.

"Hey, yourself," Elizabeth answered.

Ruby reached across the bar to touch her closest friend's

hand.

"Oh, pfff," Elizabeth snorted, insisting with that simple sound that a blubbery reunion was unnecessary. She raised her champagne flute to her lips.

"To the ghosts of Christmases past," Walter bellowed.

They all burst into applause. Ruby clapped, then swiped a tear from a cheek.

How could it be this easy? After all this time, she had stumbled onto the solution to her loneliness.

At the end of the night, empty glasses were simply placed on tabletops. Chairs screeched backward as the Christmas Eve guests began to rise and make their way across the floor, toward various exits.

"Wait, wait," Ruby cried out. "You're not leaving, are you? Elizabeth? Are you going, too?"

But Elizabeth, it seemed, was already gone. The only sign left of her was the red lipstick stain at the top of her glass.

"What'd you expect, Rubes, that we'd live here?" Walter chuckled.

"Well—no—but—?"

"We'll see you tomorrow," Walter assured her.

"Tomorrow?"

"What's a happy hour without regulars?" Walter asked with a wink. And he slipped away, through the kitchen door.

11.

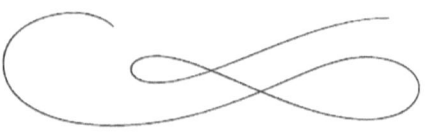

2018

"NICE move, inviting Rob to work the grand opening," Aunt Elizabeth said from behind Angela's shoulder.

Angela jumped at the sound of her voice, swiveling to find that Elizabeth was far from the only figure inside Ruby's Place. In fact, a crowd had begun to infiltrate the bar.

"He's your ticket to getting this old bar off the ground," Ruby agreed as she tossed Rob's empty beer bottle into the trash, then dropped his dirtied plates into a plastic tub.

"Absolutely." Elizabeth made her way toward her usual stool as Ruby poured her a champagne. "You heard everything Rob said," she added, tracing the rim of her glass with a fingertip. "That's one heartsick young man."

"Heartsick?" Angela repeated. But it didn't seem that either Elizabeth or Ruby heard her. The crowd had drowned her out. Not that Angela minded. This was, in fact, her favorite sight in the world: the regulars showing up for happy hour—as they always did, every single evening once the construction crews had knocked off for the day and the coast was clear.

"Never thought that Rob kid was going to get out of here," Walter grumbled as he carried one of the chairs from storage into the bar. He stood a moment, searching for a decent place to put his seat in the midst of the snaking coils of electrical cords and drills lying asleep on their sides. A place where he wouldn't bump into the ladders and paint cans.

Unlike Walter, most of the regulars were fine with sitting on the rungs of ladders or the slick top of the bar or peeling back the tarps and propping themselves on the piano bench—or, even, taking a seat on top of the piano itself.

Angela sighed, staring at them all. Yet again, she was struck by how much they gave the bar the appearance of an expensive costume party: Walter sporting sideburns and the wide suit lapels. The pianist decked out in her short sequined jacket with the batwing sleeves and a pair of bell bottoms. The Nehru collars, the Vidal Sassoon bobs of the 1960s, the '50s-era crinolines. The fancy hats, the dress gloves and stockings, the platform shoes. Each wore what had been the epitome of fashion during their own heyday.

For her part, Ruby was clad in her signature black wide-legged pants—full enough to pass for a long skirt. Her thick brunette hair had been twisted into a bun secured high on her head. Her lithe, former-ballerina body swirled between tables and sawhorses and step ladders. She hoisted a giant tray of cocktails shoulder-height while reciting, "Welcome to Ruby's, where the 'spirits' are not confined to the liquors behind the bar."

The crowd cheered, clapping and grabbing their usuals from her tray, clinking their glasses and making toasts.

"To the ghosts of Christmas past!" Walter bellowed, as he did each and every night. It was the secret Angela had stumbled upon last year. Ruby's Place was still inhabited by the spirits of those who had once flocked to the supper club to celebrate every one of their own life's triumphs.

"Everyone seems especially happy tonight," Angela remarked.

"Of course they are, dear. Ruby's is on its way back," Elizabeth said. "Don't you know we celebrated last year, the same night you happened back into the bar?" She pointed to a nearby stool, wordlessly asking that she take up the seat beside her.

Angela propped herself onto the stool, soaking up Elizabeth's appearance. Looking at Elizabeth was like thumbing through the pages of fashion magazines. That evening, Elizabeth had chosen a figure-flattering green jersey dress with a large enamel brooch and a green cocktail ring on her left hand. Her signature red lipstick and nail polish shimmered in the soft light coming from the one working overhead light. Between the polish and the ring and the giant shiny brooch, she looked a bit like a disco ball. Angela loved it. She remembered her youthful dream of growing up to be a disco ball herself.

"You—you celebrated?" Angela asked. "Just because I showed up?"

"Of course. You were the answer to our prayers. For so long, we'd been chasing all the wrong owners away from the place—making sure mold or bees infiltrated the walls, constantly undoing every single one of some poor plumber's fixes. Discouraging them with pipes that never stopped dripping or worse. Bleeding every pocketbook dry. Making sure they'd give up on the place. But when you arrived—someone who remembered the bar fondly, someone who maybe even needed us as much as we needed you—we knew that there was finally hope. You'd reopen the place in a way that would tap into the Christmas spirit rather than tear it apart. Finally, the right owner had arrived."

"I'm not anything special," Angela muttered. "It's this

place that's special."

"But you see it," Elizabeth said. "You see me—and Ruby—and the rest of our happy hour bunch. Not everyone does. It takes a special kind of person to see things in a certain way."

Angela wasn't sure about all that. So far, she mostly felt like a deadline-missing screw-up. Which did not exactly bode well for Christmas Eve.

She did know, though, that things looked different when your perspective shifted with distance or time. The way Angela viewed Aunt Elizabeth had evolved. Elizabeth had always been beautiful, but she had also been stuck in Angela's mind as an older woman. Here she was, looking exactly as she had when Angela was little—complete with crow's feet and hair that was a dyed blond to cover the gray patches. Angela was herself both grayer and heavier than she would have liked. She had age spots on her hands and indentions in the skin around her mouth. Creases in her forehead. These days, gazing at her favorite person through her own fifty-plus-year-old eyes, Aunt Elizabeth didn't look old to Angela at all.

As Elizabeth and Ruby chatted, Angela wound up thinking, once more, about how this whole buying Ruby's thing had started—last year, mere days from Christmas. It had all been a complete accident, a passerby knocking her into the door of the old bar hard enough to jar it open. Intrigued by voices, Angela had stepped inside to see it all for herself, wondering how the place could have been reopened without her hearing of it somewhere. She'd been living far enough away to miss a few ads, but why hadn't her sister told her during one of her lengthy emails or phone calls, the ones in which she breathlessly filled Angela in on the comings and goings of Sullivan?

In her confusion, Angela had seen her fabulous Aunt Elizabeth, who had passed away when Angela was still in high school—sitting on the barstool beside her, dressed to the nines.

They had talked. And it had been more delicious than the marshmallows or the cocoa she remembered from the Christmas Eves they'd shared at Ruby's Place.

"If I hadn't left my hat inside," Angela reminded Elizabeth now, "I would have talked myself out of what I'd seen. I was already doing just that. I started as soon as I stepped outside the bar again—I told myself none of it could have been true. That you were nothing more than a figment of my imagination. That I couldn't have even been inside. When I looked through the window, though, there it was—my dumb old brown hat, the one I'd taken off and laid on the bar. Seeing that convinced me that I really had been inside, and that I'd seen you."

Elizabeth nodded. "Yes, dear, I was there. I remember."

"You sure you want to put your trust in someone whose belief is dependent on some silly brown hat?"

"Are you really that worried about Christmas Eve?" Ruby asked, placing her elbows on the bar and leaning toward Angela.

"Of course she's worried," Elizabeth said through a half-grin. "It's quite a tall order."

"A place to see your long-lost loved one one last time," Ruby recited. "A chance to say everything you didn't get to say when they were alive, to right wrongs, to mend grudges. The ultimate Christmas wish."

"Yes," Elizabeth agreed, her eyes misty. "We can give that to people. It'll all begin this Christmas Eve."

"What if no one else sees?" Angela asked. "What if no one has some kind of proof, like I did? What if everyone convinces themselves it's made up, like I almost did?"

Ruby and Elizabeth exchanged knowing glances.

"I hate it when you guys do that," Angela barked. "I'm not a kid anymore. I think I can officially handle whatever it is you're keeping from me."

"*I'm* not keeping anything from you," Ruby said in falsetto, feigning innocence.

"Me, neither," Elizabeth chimed in, taking another sip of her champagne and then pretending to be completely absorbed in inspecting her manicure.

Angela slumped beneath the weight of being the one responsible for all those Christmas wishes coming true. So far, all she'd managed to produce was a half-finished renovation, which meant she wasn't even doing half as good a job as Ruby did back in the '50s, when she bought the old speakeasy. Angela had all the help in the world—the former owner and an entire town's worth of spirits on her side—and she was still fighting plumbing issues. She had no idea why the regulars weren't utterly frantic at this point.

If she could have asked for anything that holiday, it would have been for a double dose of Elizabeth's confidence. She wished she were the kind of woman who breezed into a room, always poised. A real Lauren Bacall type. Tough and elegant and ready for anything the world wanted to pummel her with.

"Pfff," Elizabeth said, reading Angela's discomfort. "Everything's going to work out. Trust us."

"And if there was any sliver of doubt before today," Ruby chimed in, "there isn't anymore. Now that you've got Rob for opening night."

Angela shook her head. "What are you guys *talking* about? What does Rob have to do with any of this?"

"First love," Ruby said simply. "We've all had one.

Didn't you?"

"Of course," Angela replied. A first love that had culminated in an engagement, as she'd told Rob, but no trip to the altar. She hated talking about it. The end was so terribly nasty, so filled with hateful remarks and accusations, that Angela had a hard time remembering her former fiancé with any fondness at all.

Ruby nudged Elizabeth.

"What?" Elizabeth grumbled, frowning at Ruby, who was pointing a finger and laughing.

"You had one, too. Or so I've heard," she teased her longtime friend.

"Yes, well. Not your typical first love," Elizabeth admitted.

"That's what makes it even better." Ruby raised an eyebrow and pursed her lips.

Elizabeth let out another dismissive "Pfff."

Angela leaned closer to her, refusing to let her simply wave it away. "I've never heard about this," she said.

"And you're not going to now," Elizabeth barked.

"Why not?" Angela pressed.

"He came along in my second act, too," Elizabeth said. "Just like the dress shop. *Late in life*. There. Okay? Isn't that enough?"

"No love at all until the second act?" Angela asked.

Elizabeth sighed with exasperation. "There had been beaus, of course. But that, for me, was the first time for the shake-you-to-your-core love. I'd never felt like that. So even though I was significantly matured, it was the first."

"Who was he?" Angela pressed. "It was someone right here in Sullivan, wasn't it? While you owned your dress shop?"

Elizabeth nodded, sinking into the cushion of a memory. "There is," she said, "nothing quite as untamed as a man falling in love. And when a girl feels it too, it whisks her up in a frenzied, all-encompassing blur. *Whirlwind.* There's a reason that word is used in romance novels."

Elizabeth cleared her throat and straightened up, reaching for her drink in a way that announced she'd obviously said all she would on the matter. Case closed, none of anybody's business, discussion over.

"How about you?" Angela asked Ruby.

"Oh, I had beaus, too," Ruby answered, smiling softly. "But I never loved anything in this world as much as I loved this place."

Ruby downed the last of her whiskey sour in one gulp. After clanking her glass on the bar, she admitted, with the slightest touch of sadness lacing her tone, "You tell somebody a business, a brick and mortar place, was the love of your life, and they look at you like somehow, you're cold. There's something wrong with your heart. You were the type of girl who couldn't commit—couldn't properly love another person. But this business brought me the most amazing friends through the years. And this place brought them all back to me. It even brought me you," she said, patting Angela's shoulder. "And now, *now*, with your help, Ruby's Place is getting a new life—a second wind. Imagine all the new faces that we'll be greeting this Christmas Eve."

Angela frowned. There it was again: Christmas Eve. The fun of sharing love-life details waned, allowing for her growing panic to return. "I still don't understand how you believe this thing will come together," she admitted.

"How is it not utterly clear?" Ruby asked, the shock in her voice making her words louder than they needed to be.

"What don't you understand, dear?" Elizabeth asked.

"The goal is to reopen Ruby's year-round, as Sullivan's newest hot spot. And on Christmas Eve, we'll allow those with an open heart to have one last moment with someone they've been missing. Closure. A chance to say things that never got said. The lovely welcoming atmosphere will keep new customers coming all year long. But the idea that this old bar might be— well, *haunted*—or at the very least, home to weird goings-on— will continue to bring people out in droves on Christmas Eve.

Hoping for their own shot at a reunion. Right?"

Elizabeth and Ruby eyed her in a way that said she was far slower to catching on than they'd thought.

"So what does Rob being my door greeter have to do with any of it?" Angela asked again, her hands out, palm up. Pleading for an answer.

The two women grinned at each other.

"You've got to jump-start this thing," Ruby said. "Get people to come for the first Christmas Eve to ensure they'll continue to come every year thereafter. Rob offers the promise of a first-love reunion. Between two hometown kids everyone remembers fondly—and still talks about. One who lives here, the other who's back home, for less than happy reasons. You've got a full-blown tear-jerker in the making. That'll draw the people of Sullivan out. You're guaranteed to have a full house and then some on Christmas Eve. All you have to do is get both Rob and Geena here. You're halfway to that goal already. You've got him. Now, you just need to work on her."

"But how will everyone else know they'll be here?"

Again, the two women grinned at each other. And at the same time, they both said, "Gossip."

12.

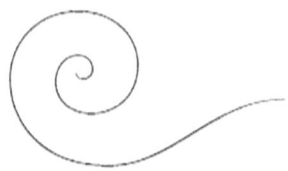

"I need a new book," Geena's father announced as she re-filled his nightstand water glass.

"Yeah?" she asked, tucking his blanket tighter. It was good to hear him make requests—for books, for a grilled cheese sandwich (cheddar cheese, on rye, skiff of mustard). Good to get into arguments with him over what to watch on TV. When he'd first come home, he'd been so innervated, he'd barely even had the strength to grunt or blink, much less form a coherent opinion.

"What do you feel like?" She smiled down at him. She didn't literally think of what had taken place between the two of them as a role-reversal, not like she suspected her father did. She simply saw it as someone she loved needing some help. When people you cared about needed you, it felt good to pitch in. It had felt good to help her fellow teacher friend Sally move into her new townhouse. It had felt good to take up the slack in the English Department's main office when the dean of the College of Arts and Letters had waddled off to have her baby. And it felt good now—better than all those other instances combined—to keep her childhood home tidy, to run her father's errands and pay his bills, and to make sure his world did not fall apart while he recuperated.

She'd made sure the house was festive, too. Their tree was down from the attic, sparkling in the living room at that very moment. Metal poinsettias lined the front walk. A wreath of tiny silver bells adorned the front door. Before New Year's rolled around, she'd have all their decorations boxed back up and stacked tidily in storage.

When her father regained his strength, he would simply step back into life as it had been, nothing to clean or catch up on. And that would make Geena feel good, too. Proud. Like she had finally done something important for the man who had done tens of thousands of important things for her.

She shook her wavy blond hair away from her face and pushed her glasses back up her nose. She wouldn't have been caught dead in glasses when she was younger, but she had hit the *I am what I am* phase of life. She had a Dr. in front of her name. She taught literature. Every single room in her apartment had bookcases filled to overflowing—so many of them, she had no wall space left over for art. It was silly to pretend that she wasn't a bookish sort, and that she hadn't wrecked her eyes in the process.

She sat on the edge of his bed and crossed her legs, her knee jutting through a tear in her favorite jeans. She'd read someplace that the things you became attached to as a teenager were the things you held on to the longest: girls continued to draw their eyeliner the same way they had at sixteen, men followed the same sports teams they'd begun watching since before they could drive. A person's favorite song usually released during their high school years.

And now, here she was in a pair of torn jeans—one of the few articles of clothing she'd grabbed and tossed in her duffel bag before boarding a flight to come home. It was goofy, she knew. She was too old for ripped jeans. Geena wasn't exactly glued to *Vogue*, but she figured that by now, in the fashion world, ripped jeans had to be as passé as perms and blue eyeshadow. She couldn't help it. She loved ripped jeans.

"I bought a bunch of new books at the airport," Geena said. "I bet I have something…"

"Noooot your books," Tom begged. "Please."

"What's wrong with my books?"

"Too slow. Too highbrow. I want a good story."

"A story, eh? By that, do you mean a Western?"

"Yeah. Good idea!" he offered, still somewhat weakly,

as though that wasn't where he'd been headed all along.

"Have you ever heard of this guy, let me see if I can remember his name…" Geena tapped her chin. "Hmmm. Louie…Lasoure, I think. No—Lagore. Lawore. That's it, isn't it? Ring any bells?"

"Ha-ha," he grumbled. They both knew he'd read everything L'Amour had written roughly fourteen times.

His eyelids began drooping.

Geena's smile faded. He may have regained his opinions on literature, but his stamina was still eluding him.

Growing up, Geena'd thought of her father as made of the toughest stuff on the planet. Not just strong and manly, but downright impenetrable—torn straight from the pages of one of his L'Amour sagas, with a tough-guy mustache that went perfectly well with his police officer uniform. Back when Geena still wore contacts and ripped jeans were not passé, she'd been the girl whose father was no one to mess with, muscled and imposing and yet unwaveringly fair. Geena had worried about nothing when he was around.

Seeing him after he had taken such a massive hit had been a blow of its own, knocking the air out of her.

"I'll download you one," Geena said, and leaned forward, starting to get up.

"No!" her dad cried, grabbing her arm. His grip was as

sure and severe as it had ever been. That pleased Geena. "You cannot read Westerns on a computer screen," Tom contended. "It's totally bizarre, incompatible. Sacrilegious, even."

"Getting a little over the top, there. And besides, you're not reading the Western; I am. I'll be reading out loud—and with the proper Western accent, thank you very much—because your eyes still get tired. Right?"

"Bah! No downloading! You'll have L'Amour rolling in his grave."

"Maybe it's time to update. Give an e-book a shot. Or—here's something—switch up genres, for once. Find a new hero."

"Oh, really? *You* think I should update? Dr. Barister, professor of Renaissance poetry and heavy metal on vinyl?"

"Dad—"

"Aren't you the one who lectured me on how you were never ever going to stop listening to your favorite bands on your vintage turntable? What happened to that iPod thing I bought you for your birthday a hundred years ago? It's in your junk drawer with the broken shoelaces and the dried-up pens, isn't it? Did you ever put a single song on it?"

Geena sighed. "Fine," she said, in the same way she'd said it when she was sixteen: *Fiiiiiine.*

"And what about your own reading collection? Huh?"

Tom went on. "Don't you have hundreds of print books on your shelves? Weren't you the same person that said e-books were a method of last resort? Something you read when stranded on a desert island with no library in six thousand miles?"

She stuck her tongue out, as she always did when her dad won an argument. "You sleep. I'll go grab a copy. I bet Walmart—"

"No!" he shouted again. "Not Walmart. The Page Turner."

"Walmart's closer. I'm sure they have a perfectly respectable Western or two."

"The Page Turner," he insisted. "They've got a great Westerns section."

"Since when? They used to have a crummy section. You said so yourself."

"That was when you were a kid. Got new ownership now. Much better. Order my Westerns special for me. I have a whole shelf there all my own."

"Do you."

"Yes. They'll know what I haven't read yet. Or lately."

"Dad, that's really cool, but listen, Walmart's a ten minute trip and—"

"The Page Turner."

"I don't want to leave you alone that long."

"I'm going to be asleep," he said, his voice low and thick. Grabbing her arm like he had, arguing with her, seemed to have drained him completely. He was already starting to drift off. "Trust me. I'll sleep while you're gone, and then I'll be ready for a story when you get back. You can sit right here," he murmured, pointing to the chair beside his bed, "and stay awhile." His eyes drifted shut.

Geena smiled, pushing a lock of white hair across his forehead. It was the phrase she most often associated with her father: *Stay awhile*, which she'd heard directed at neighbors and fellow police officers and old friends all through her childhood. *Stay awhile*, which she still heard him say to her, now that she was grown, usually while he was tucking a plane ticket with her name on it into her bag—a free ride back to Sullivan and him.

"What if you need something while I'm not here? Dad?"

"I won't."

"I'm getting Mrs. Cranston from next door."

"No babysitters," he growled, his eyes popping back open.

"It's Walmart or Cranston. One or the other. Which one is more important?"

"The Page Turner, little girl," he managed. "Believe me, what I want is there."

13.

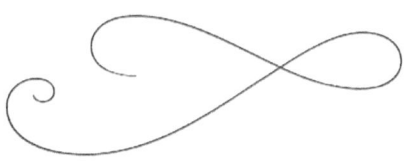

"ARE you sure it's okay?" Geena pressed, standing on Mrs. Cranston's porch. "You're not just saying that, are you?"

She was a sweet old neighbor, Mrs. Cranston, the kind that had once filled the screens of black-and-white sitcoms. A middle-aged widow with no children and a warm heart, always there should Geena and Tom need a cup of sugar or someone to collect their mail while on vacation. They had keys to each other's front doors and were listed as each other's emergency contacts. Tom had answered a few midnight phone calls through the years, racing into the Cranston house to hunt down the source of strange noises: usually overgrown tree branches scraping a window or, once, a family of squirrels burrowing in her attic.

When Geena was seven, she'd spent nearly an entire summer in the Cranston kitchen with its olive green tile, learning how to bake. Mrs. Cranston must have nearly gone broke buying all the ingredients for lattice crusts or cinnamon rolls or carrot cake, a different recipe every day. Geena's parents had recently divorced, and Mrs. Cranston and her flour sifter had been how Geena had mourned the loss of her family. Breaking up, she'd learned that summer, was a kind of death. Your world wasn't the same afterward.

She'd learned it again, in another way, when she knew Rob was gone for good.

"I hate to ask," Geena admitted. "It's such a silly thing. I made sure to have the week's groceries delivered so I wouldn't have to leave him alone, and now he decides he needs something to read. I mean, I could have downloaded something new, but he wants a Louis L'Amour. And he says—"

"—you can't read a Western on a screen," Mrs. Cranston finished. She flicked a dishtowel at Geena. "Scat, scat, you get out and take your time. Blow the dust off."

Geena laughed—Mrs. Cranston used to say that during their baking summer, when she wanted her to go outside and play. *Go blow the dust off.* Only this time, her neck kind of jiggled when she flicked the towel. And it struck Geena that Mrs. Cranston had gotten old in the time that had elapsed since their weeks of vinegar pie and tomato soup spice cake. She was smaller than she used to be, her body like a balloon that was slowly leaking air.

And her father was upstairs in her childhood home, asleep in the middle of the day, recovering from a heart attack.

The second hands weren't ticking off actual seconds, but weeks. With every single flick.

"He's asleep right now," Geena said. "He shouldn't be any trouble. I didn't want him to be alone…"

"Gives me a chance to catch up on my knitting," Mrs. Cranston said. She raced to grab her needles and yarn.

"Here," Geena said, pressing a folded piece of paper toward Mrs. Cranston. "It's my cell number. If anything at all changes—"

"We'll be fine. Never you worry," Mrs. Cranston assured her.

And because it was coming from the same woman who had made her world feel not quite so destroyed that summer after her parents' divorce, Geena believed her.

She thanked Mrs. Cranston three more times as the two women headed in two different directions, Mrs. Cranston to Geena's house and Geena toward her dad's car, the 2014 Impala.

And that was that.

Or so Geena thought.

14.

THE angry clatter of a bus grinding to a stop bled through the front window of The Page Turner. Rob cringed, covering his ears with his hands until the screech died down.

He sighed, wondering if a fancier store might have tougher, more soundproof plate glass. His store was as far from fancy as it could get. No coffee or pretty bookmarks, no artisanal snacks or mugs with catchy sayings or coloring books or silly calligraphy pens—the kind of things that were purchased as gifts and never used, not once, just tossed in a drawer and forgotten.

The Page Turner sold books, nothing more. According to Rob, books were the top of the food chain. The Taj Mahal. The *Mona Lisa*. Artisanal snacks and coloring books could not compare to the *Mona Lisa*.

Outside, the bus coughed, sending a gray cloud of fumes through the air. The engine roared as it pulled away from the curb, slinging hammers into his headache. He rubbed his temples, finding no relief. Justin was out of school that day— teachers' workday—but Rob still wasn't sure if he'd show up to help or not. He wished the kid would hurry up and text him already. He needed him. He'd bought an entire collection earlier that morning from a woman paring down for an out-of-state move: five giant boxes of hardback books, most of them first editions, a few of them signed. Inventory was always a pain, and by that point, two hours into it, he was pretty much convinced he'd never get to the bottom of it all.

"These books are multiplying inside the cardboard box-es," he announced.

"Must be some hot romances in there," Kelly, his one and only employee, joked.

Rob laughed, and instantly regretted it. His own voice echoed in his head—each tiny sound creating a spiral of painful throbs.

He was exhausted, having slept less than two hours, and he was plain hungover. He rarely drank at all anymore—it seemed ridiculous and childish, like suddenly deciding to sport a green mohawk at fifty. Still, for some reason, he'd wound up downing four of the beers that Angela had given him the night before.

Mostly, he'd drunk them in an attempt to stop thinking about what he'd overheard in the checkout line at the grocery store.

Why had some silly gossipy tidbit been so unsettling? Why was he so rattled? It couldn't be because they'd spoken of Geena. He'd certainly heard her name more than once, more than often since returning to Sullivan.

Had it been because Tom'd had a heart attack? Was that why he was upset? Tom was going to be fine. That was what everyone kept repeating. Was it because he couldn't make up his mind about whether or not it was a good idea to ring the man's doorbell? *Go see Tom or don't go.* Why was it such a hard decision?

Wait—hadn't he decided last night? Hadn't he already told Angela he wasn't going through with it?

Then why did it feel so uncertain? If the decision had been made, why was he still thinking about it?

He glanced up at the poster of Hemingway he had acquired at a book fair, hanging near the checkout counter. He couldn't advertise Godiva chocolate he didn't sell, after all. He had to advertise the one product he did offer: books. Classics. Contemporaries. First editions. He wanted hardcore readers. He'd been convinced that hanging Papa where he'd be visible from the street would do the trick.

Now, though, Papa was shooting him what he interpreted to be a decidedly disparaging look. *Have you seen your-self?* the look said. *Hungover at work. Pathetic.* Rob made a face back and grumbled, "You're one to talk."

Now that he was looking, though, he realized Hemingway had been hanging up long enough to be nearly completely bleached by the sun. Rob chastised himself for thumbtacking Papa too close to the front window. He probably should have switched the poster out for another—one of the authors he personally loved. Ursula K. Le Guin, maybe. William Gibson. Kurt Vonnegut. Somehow, though, at this point, he didn't have the heart to take it down.

Maybe he'd always been like that. Maybe he hung on to things too long.

His head clattered and banged.

He needed food. A decent lunch. That would help his hangover.

He circled out from behind the counter and tried to follow the sounds Kelly was making as she shelved new arrivals. Ah, Kelly, his ever-faithful employee, supplementing her retirement income. His overly sensitive ears perked. Which aisle was she in? Historical Fiction? Poetry? Children's? *Mystery.*

He veered toward the aisle and smiled when he saw her, a stout woman on a step stool. *Stout.* He liked the word, even though it was probably old-fashioned enough to have grown a bit offensive.

"Kelly," he said. "Lunch."

"Plain baked potato and a Diet Pepsi," she ordered, handing him a few folded dollar bills from her cardigan pocket. To his teasing look of disgust, she smiled and used her free hand to pat her thigh, hidden for the most part beneath a shapeless dress.

He felt bad for that *stout* thing.

But he managed a smile and said with a wave, "Back in ten."

Kelly's lips wiggled. Her lips always wiggled while shelving books. She pushed aside some titles on the top shelf, and slid a Mary Higgins Clark into the hole she'd just made. Glancing over her shoulder, she called back, "You can take twenty if it'll make that potato taste like pumpkin pie."

15.

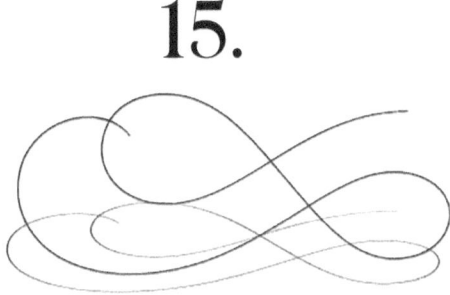

GEENA had nearly made it all the way to The Page Turner when she realized she was about to get run over. By a skateboarder, no less. Yes, here she was, right across the street, The Page Turner's electric sign in sight, and before she could finish her errand, she was going to get absolutely clobbered.

She darted, saving herself from the young man weaving his bright red and yellow board back and forth. He zigzagged and hopped over holes and cracks in the sidewalk, ears plugged with earbuds, chanting along loudly to whatever song he was listening to. He had no idea how close they'd both come to turning into a skinned, bruised heap on the pavement.

Geena watched, startled when he suddenly whipped back around. She yelped, but he continued singing off-key without a hiccup, eyes on his feet. How could she get his attention if he couldn't hear her? And when had she stopped being able to instantly recognize the latest popular songs?

She jerked back and forth, trying to figure out which direction she needed to go to keep her toes from being smashed by his wheels. How strange, she caught herself thinking as she watched him, that the jeans-slung-low-on-the-hips thing never died. But then again, she told herself, it kind of justified her being out in her own ripped Levi's, didn't it? She stood there, hugging her vintage man's wool Pendleton jacket tightly around her middle, marveling at how easily the boy manipulated the board, and then watching in amazement as he did one of his tricks, flipping the board and catching it again with his feet. He stopped, then suddenly zipped back toward her, hypnotizing her with his spinning yellow wheels.

No. She couldn't be hypnotized. She needed to snap out of it. He still didn't see her. Of that, she was certain. How could he be so oblivious?

She kept her eyes on the front of his skateboard, those wheels the color of caution signs, looking for some indication as to which direction he'd be headed next. And because she was so focused on his path, she finally saw it: The inscribed square. Her name and Rob's.

Geena cocked her head.

The boy veered, and she hopped out of his way. Maybe she and the young man weren't going to run into each other, but the inscription had just crashed into her, nearly knocking her to the ground.

She had forgotten—or, really, simply tucked it away, stopped thinking of it long enough ago that it surprised her now. In a whir that passed as quickly as one turn of the boy's skateboard wheels, she was jarred by the sight, then warmed by it. Good grief, for a split second, she was proud. Like maybe she'd walked upon her own name on a marquee.

That was her down there, in the sidewalk. Her carefree, in-love, teenage self, anyway. Seemed like another lifetime.

The engraving had found its own way to fade, Geena noticed—the deep indentions of the letters had been filled in with bits and scraps of wrappers and receipts, crumbled leaves, chewed-up bubblegum, rained-on cigarette butts, and the dirt kicked up by tennis shoes and bicycle tires.

The words were far from illegible, but they had certainly aged—every bit as much as Mrs. Cranston had, every bit as much as her father. Every bit as much as Geena.

And Rob. He had to have aged, too.

The boy roared back yet again, wrapped in a *woosh* that whisked Geena back to the day she'd stood on this very corner, laughing hard enough that she had to fight for her breath. (Had it really seemed funny to her, though, or had she only wanted to get everyone's attention? Had she decided to be the kind of loud that dared people to stop and look at what was going on?) Laughing as Rob had scratched their names into the freshly poured sidewalk: one part cement, two parts sand, three parts gravel, and one hundred percent permanent. At not-quite-sixteen, it was better than a marriage proposal.

It was bold. *Wild*, that was the word she'd used then.

Maybe, when you were sixteen, it didn't take much for someone to seem wild. Long hair, a stolen shot glass tied to a rearview mirror with a scrunchie. A scratch of mostly harmless graffiti.

Geena closed her eyes and began to peel back the layers of time that had passed: so many schools, so many classrooms, the years lived in one-hour segments. English 101, Victorian Lit Survey, pages and pages of print.

She'd learned to arrange her own bookshelves away from the sun in her office. Sun wrecked them.

Everything faded, after all. Print and dust jackets and... affection. That faded, too. She'd seen it time and again with the men who'd come and gone.

But before it all, before college and her graduate studies and receiving her title—Dr.—before any of that, there had been a boy with long hair, a boy who made her feel alive and reckless and free, and he had written a declaration of love where everyone could see it, on the most bustling corner in downtown Sullivan, Missouri.

16.

NGELA'S pulse thundered far harder inside her ears than the nail guns had moments ago.

The bar was almost eerily quiet. The work crew had broken for lunch, leaving Angela to pore over the stack of bills with due dates growing ever closer.

But Angela wasn't alone.

In the front window, Angela could see her own hazy reflection alongside the hazier reflections belonging to Elizabeth and Ruby.

"Look," Angela whispered, pointing at Geena, who was silently staring down at the sidewalk square bearing her name. She dragged her finger across the glass, toward The Page Turner, where Rob stood beside the entrance, first rubbing his temples, then reaching into a coat pocket and pulling out a pair of gloves.

"Do they see each other?" Angela hissed at her partners. "They don't, do they? Shouldn't they?"

Neither Elizabeth nor Ruby answered.

But Angela couldn't simply stand by and do nothing. How could Elizabeth and Ruby expect her to? This was torture. Besides, the bar regulars had never just sat back and waited. They'd driven off the wrong owners. They'd kept their secret from the wrong people.

Elizabeth and Ruby had told her that Rob and Geena would draw crowds on Christmas Eve. She had to make sure they would come.

She lunged toward the door.

Which was suddenly, strangely locked.

It had to be locked. Why else would she be unable to turn the knob?

"It's not our time to get involved," Ruby told her, drawing her away from the door.

"How can you be sure?" Angela asked, her shoes scraping against the floor.

"Trust me," Ruby assured her, bringing her back to the window. "Right now, we need to watch."

17.

GEENA couldn't put her finger on why, but the skater reminded her of Rob. It could have been his age, and the fact that she had seconds ago seen Rob's name on the sidewalk square. But on second glance, she swore all he needed was longer hair, maybe some high-top Converse sneakers, and he would have been a dead ringer.

It was a little spooky. The longer Geena stared at the skater, the closer yesterday felt. All of it. Rob and the day he'd carved their names into that sidewalk and who she'd been at sixteen.

Maybe it was just being home again. Sleeping in her old room, the same one she used to smuggle Rob into after dark.

And maybe it was coming face-to-face with how much time had passed. Maybe it was seeing that time had no compassion, not even for fathers who were as tough as the heroes of

Louis L'Amour books.

She smiled at the sidewalk square, liking that although it had faded, it wasn't gone, not completely.

Still life left in it yet. That was something Mrs. Cranston might have said. It was true for the sidewalk, and it was true of other things Geena loved and wasn't ready to let go of—especially her father.

"This is silly," Geena chastised herself.

She checked her phone, surprised to find she'd already been gone twenty minutes. Guilt lit a flame inside her. Mrs. Cranston had told her, "Take your time." But maybe she was trying to be overly nice to the poor girl whose dad had suffered a heart attack. Besides, after ten minutes on Tom's lumpy leather living room chair, with little more than a myriad of sports channels to keep her company while she knitted, Mrs. Cranston was bound to get sick of father-sitting fairly quickly. She was also bound to wonder if Geena's trip was dragging on long enough to border on her being taken advantage of.

Geena didn't want Mrs. Cranston to think badly of her. She loved Mrs. Cranston, even now. When her heart latched onto something worthy of the slightest bit of attention, it sunk in its tentacles and refused to let go. It had always been that way for her.

Why was she wasting time standing and staring at this

kid with his skateboard? Playing some pointless Memory Lane game with herself?

The chilly winter breeze punished her with a slap on her cheek. She deserved it. She needed to get a move on. And come to think of it, what if the store didn't even have any L'Amours? Why hadn't she called ahead of time? Why had she taken her father's word for it?

Because he'd been so adamant. A shelf all his own, he'd said. "New owner," he'd repeated through a smile. Thinking about it now, Geena swore he'd been happier telling her about The Page Turner than he'd been about anything since he'd gotten home from the hospital.

No daughter would have been able to argue with such enthusiasm.

Hopefully, Mrs. Cranston, once a daughter herself, would understand.

18.

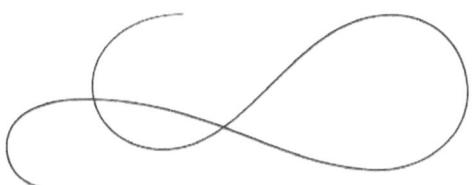

ROB glanced across the street, happy to see his son on his skateboard. He waved, but wasn't sure Justin saw him.

His head was killing him, keeping him from thinking in a straight line. He caught himself mulling over silly things, relatively unimportant things, routine things—like lunch. Kelly's plain baked potato and the potato he would get, with broccoli and cheese. His mind ran over a few semi-more-important things, too, like maybe getting Justin to come to the diner with him. Take-out for three. And how he might con Justin into admitting he had a girlfriend—a Geena of his own. Oh, he was a lucky boy, if he was in that period of life—if he had found his Geena, his first love. Justin wouldn't realize his luck. Boys his age never did.

Maybe, after lunch, he could wrangle Justin into helping him finish cataloging all those books stacked in the store.

His hangover propelled his fuzzy mind into an even stranger, disordered cluster of thoughts. How people in the midst of moving had become his bread and butter, for instance. They always came in to dump their volumes at his bookstore. People could always unload their favorites when push got to shove. No one wanted to lug around a heavy pile of books forever.

Rob was the one who hung on to things too long: his faded Hemingway poster, his ratty old Royals hat. The gossip—Tom's heart attack, Geena being back in town—was making him realize he'd held a few memories close, too. Longer than he should have.

What was the point of thinking of Geena? Of that silly sidewalk square? When he was Justin's age, he'd played a game with himself every time Geena had wandered into his daydreams. Kind of a *Wonder if she's thinking about me right, now, too?* Back then, he'd sworn two people thinking of each other at the same time was a kind of dance—only with your fantasies in sync instead of your feet.

And wasn't that really the best dance of all?

But it was time to stop playing that game. It was time to move on. For once. Hang a new poster. Get a new Royals hat. Stop bringing up the same childish thoughts. Toss out a few things that had faded beyond recognition.

Surely, by now, Geena had. Why think of someone else when they'd long stopped thinking of you?

Rob tried to motion for Justin to come on, hurry up, cross the street.

But he stopped when he realized someone else was standing on the sidewalk near Justin.

Someone he would have recognized anywhere.

19.

GEENA couldn't quit staring at the skater, even though she was beginning to feel a little weird about it. Years ago, a boy like that would have been flattered to find her staring—no, no, *had* been flattered. Years ago, her stare had made Rob walk right up to her and flirt, start the whole thing between them rolling. Now, though, she was too old for staring at boys. At her age, staring had a creepy connotation. She knew that, and still, she couldn't stop. And she couldn't shake the strange feeling that this boy reminded her of Rob.

Standing on top of her own name, near someone who made her feel close to Rob, she was engulfed by the past. By who that girl carved into the sidewalk had been—so sweet and trusting and willing to let a long-haired, wild boy wiggle all the way into her heart.

The breakup songs were true, first cut and all that.

Standing here, in the midst of the past, a strange ache opened up inside her. Geena began to suspect that her tentacle heart had never let Rob back out again.

Was she actually missing a sixteen-year-old boy who no longer existed? How ludicrous. Stupid tentacle heart.

The skateboarder whipped around, seeing Geena for the first time. He jerked to the side and bellowed, waving his arms, fighting to regain balance. Geena lunged forward; they grabbed onto each other. When the wobbling stopped, they both smiled, laughing with relief.

Face flaming pink, the boy apologized for scaring her.

And then he turned and called out to a man standing on the other side of the street—something like, *Hey* or *Coming* or just plain *Dad!* Something he'd clearly said thousands of times before.

The man waved. Haltingly, it seemed.

Now that she was looking right at him, she knew—with a greater certainty than she had ever felt before—that it was him. Rob.

A little heavier, with shorter hair, grayer hair. And not an ounce less handsome than he'd ever been.

Here I am, she wanted to cry out. *Remember me?*

Did he recognize her? Did he know who she was?

"Dad!" the boy cried out. Clearly this time.

No wonder the skater reminded her of Rob.

After the longest of pauses, after the same two kids of the *Rob & Geena 4Ever 1987* sidewalk corner fame finally pushed past a prolonged period of staring at each other in complete and total bewilderment, it happened.

One of them made the first move.

20.

KIMBERLY Tan slid a deliciously fat historical novel from the shelf in the Davis County Library only to find a pair of green eyes staring back at her.

She jumped, nearly dropping the book. Then sighed with relief when she recognized the eyes belonged to Ryan Jeffries. He had been spooking her through the library shelves since the seventh grade, back in 1989.

She expected him to snort with laughter. To say, "Still works" or "Gotcha again" as she put her hand on her chest, trying to calm her racing heart.

That day, though, neither of those things happened. Ryan's green eyes were serious. "You hear about Tom Barister?" he murmured.

Kimberly nodded, brushing her black bangs to the side of her forehead. "Yeah," she said. "I did."

"Sudden cardiac death," he said. "Brutal."

"I heard that's kind of common," Kimberly said. "You're more likely to die of sudden cardiac arrest in the first thirty days after a heart attack."

"It couldn't have been much more than a week, though," Ryan hissed. "He probably thought he'd been given this new lease on life. Like after he got through resting and recuperating, he'd have all this time."

"Bet his daughter thought so, too," Kimberly said. "You know, Geena used to babysit me when I was little, and—"

Five feet or so down the aisle, an overly loud clearing of the throat burst into the air, interrupting what was sure to be a long-winded tale. Kimberly turned to find an older man glaring at her over the top of his readers.

Eyeing Ryan again, she jerked her head to the side a couple of times, wordlessly asking him to circle around, meet her at the edge of the Historical Fiction section.

"—all I know is," Kimberly said, picking up her story as Ryan joined her and they began to walk toward the Children's section where their respective spouses and kids were attending Saturday afternoon storytime, "Geena was running an errand for Tom—went out to get him some books, I think—and before she got home, her neighbor called her, all frantic. Telling her she had to get home quick."

"Which neighbor?"

"Cranston. I think that's right. And by the time Geena got home, he was, you know—"

"Dead."

"Right."

"Brutal," he said again.

"Yeah."

"You know her well, you said? Babysitter and all that?"

Kimberly shrugged as she watched the circle of kids fidgeting through the weekend read-aloud. A few stared out the window, others played with the threads in the carpet. Ryan's son was tugging on the edge of her own daughter's pigtail, while Ryan's wife gently tried to scold his little fingers away without creating a scene. Kimberly smiled. *Like father like son.*

"Well, you know she was pretty far ahead of us in school. But like I said, she used to watch me when my parents had to go to business dinners. She always came with about fifteen different books." She shook her head, chuckling softly. "Books," she repeated, hugging her historical novel.

"Gotta be lonely in that house right now. Wonder if she kept up with the people in her class. Surely somebody's in town that can reach out to her, help her out a little. Do you know who she hung out with back then?"

Kimberly glanced up at Ryan, who had stopped, some-

where in the more than twenty years since their own graduation, looking exactly like a blond All-American football quar-
terback, and had started looking more like a bald middle-aged
gym teacher.

"Only one. But I hear they don't talk anymore. Ancient
history," she murmured.

Over in the storytime room, the librarian turned the
page and held the hardback up for all to see the illustration.
"Books," she muttered again.

21.

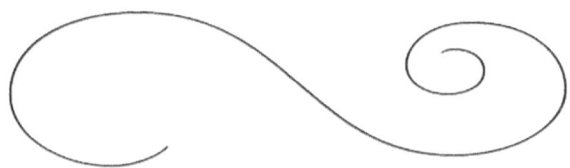

THE news of Tom's demise didn't stick to Geena's old acquaintances or the aisles of the Davis County Library. It spread like flood waters through Sullivan. It raged and poured through every neighborhood, schoolyard, book club, and bowling league. It raced straight to Angela, bursting through the entrance of Ruby's Place.

By the time the work crew left and the regulars appeared for happy hour, the floodwaters of bad news were knee deep. The dark, murky waters of despair were strong enough to make the heavy oak tables float out of storage, straight into the serving area.

"It's truly the saddest happy hour this place has ever seen," Ruby observed sourly, sloshing through the puddles of disbelief with a tray full of mixed drinks.

Not that anyone responded. No one had anything to

say. They all stared at their melting ice cubes, every single one of them thinking something along the same lines: *He was just out front on the sidewalk a few days ago. Angela and one of her builders got him to the emergency room in time. He'd been rescued—he was well enough to be released from the hospital. Why didn't the doctors have some suspicion this would happen?*

It threw everyone. Because it was a reminder that rescue was never guaranteed. Neither was success. Which meant that maybe all their own plans for Ruby's Place and the holiday—all their dreams and their visions of saving the old bar—weren't a sure thing, either.

The old sconces buzzed. The piano played a slow, sad tune.

Poor Tom. Poor Geena. And on top of it all, poor us, they thought, their expressions broadcasting anxiety.

Could Tom's sudden death foreshadow defeat for Ruby's Place?

As their fears mounted, a woman in the center of the bar stood up, holding her bottle of beer high above her head. Barbara Lewis—a tall, striking woman Angela had been introduced to nearly a year ago—wore her favorite stonewashed jeans, full through the hips and tight at the ankles. Her white blouse, complete with circa 1986 shoulder pads, offered the perfect contrast to her black shoulder-length mane and her dark skin. "To Tom," she announced, "who was there for me when I wrecked my dad's car the same night I got my driver's license. He broke the news to my dad for me, softened the blow. Made sure he knew it was a missing stop sign and not a distracted teenager that caused the accident." She dabbed at her eyes.

"Here, here," came a voice from the back of the bar.

"To Tom," another voice called out. This time, it belonged to Judy Woodward, still dressed in her favorite '60s-era Chanel-style collar-less suit, her blond hair arranged into something akin to a style Doris Day would have worn in a popular rom-com. "Tom, who helped more than one woman get out of a bad situation at home. As an old social worker, I know that firsthand."

"To Tom," announced Walter, standing and raising his shot glass. "Worst better on football in the history of all time. He personally funded three of my son's birthdays."

"To Tom!" Ruby shouted. "A great baritone! And a fan of Johnny Mercer tunes."

Laughter erupted; glasses clinked. The floodwaters of sadness and fear began to recede, bleeding out of the crack under the front door.

Angela knocked her own shot of whiskey back and thunked the glass on the bar. Suddenly, the place was filled with more stories of Tom than Aunt Elizabeth's champagne was filled with bubbles. Details swirled around her, all those pieces and bits of tales about the man who had apparently been Sullivan's favorite cop: A wild recounting of a daring rescue when the lake flooded. The night he pulled two passengers from a burning car. The mornings he served pancake breakfasts at fundraisers.

A hero, she kept hearing. *In Tom's world, there were only good guys and bad guys, and nothing in-between. In Tom's world, if you were a good guy, he'd defend you with his last breath.*

"Won't Tom be here?" Angela asked Elizabeth. "Why isn't he here now?"

Elizabeth's strained face turned pale, and she tightened her fingers around the stem of her champagne flute. "Oh, Angie," she sighed, using a nickname that Angela hadn't heard for more than forty years. "People only come if they have reason to."

"Tom didn't come to Ruby's that much?" Angela pressed. "Is that it? That's why he's not here now?"

Elizabeth's eyes grew even more distant and sad than they'd been a moment before.

Angela wasn't sure why Elizabeth seemed so caught up in her own thoughts. Then again, didn't that always happen when death got close? It made people think about themselves, create lists in their minds: what they'd accomplished, what dreams had faded, what wishes still burned bright.

Maybe, Angela thought, the same was also true for those who had their entire lives behind them.

"Tom used to come," Ruby admitted, "but he stopped…"

22.

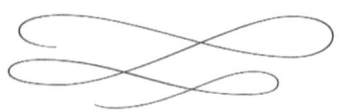

1990

TOM stepped into Ruby's still wearing his uniform. He'd never, not once, ever come into Ruby's still wearing his uniform. Heading to Ruby's meant a trip to the barbershop. It meant a new tie. It meant picking up his suit from the cleaners. It meant a shoe shine. But Tom didn't see the point in dressing up. Not that year. Who would he be dressing for?

He was having a hard time remembering the last time he'd ever spent a Christmas completely alone. Surely, though, a drop-in at Ruby's would rid him of his rotten blues.

"Hey, Tom," Ruby called out, wiping the bar down. But her voice didn't seem to have the same music in it.

He nodded, sliding onto a stool.

The old pub was decked out, like always—mistletoe

and tinsel and boughs of holly. The pianist hammered "The First Noel." The air smelled of pine and something sweet—probably Ruby's homemade marshmallows.

But Ruby's Place was mostly empty.

A man and woman sat in the back in that new-couple way—heads together, each of them struggling to get a word in edgewise—so much to tell each other, so much they agreed on, laughter bubbling.

The man wore a pair of faded jeans and an equally faded T-shirt over long-sleeved thermals, Tom noted. The woman a short skirt and a tight sweater. Nothing fancy. No gloves, no hats. No suits. Her boots were scuffed. He thought of his own shoe shine kit at home, with the saddle soaps and the various brown and black polishes and the soft rags and the brushes. Did anyone even polish their shoes anymore?

Another man sat alone, nursing a scotch. Staring out the nearby window.

The pianist finished her carol and flipped through a songbook, trying to decide on her next performance. She placed her fingers on the keys and began to play "God Rest Ye Merry, Gentlemen."

But no one sang along. No one carried their drink to the piano. No one even drummed their fingertips on their table in time to the tune or hummed or smiled at the pianist.

It's just that it's the afternoon, Tom told himself. Of course that was it.

But Tom was lying to himself. He had never been inside Ruby's during Christmas when people weren't singing along. Not even when he happened by during what should have been the after-lunch respite. Even then, it was suits and hats and singing. Even then, it was packed.

The magic of the place was gone. Because, for the most part, the people were gone. Ruby's felt like a gift of yesterday that had worn out and been relegated to some forgotten basement corner.

"Glad you stopped by," Ruby said, sliding a beer in front of Tom.

"Couldn't let Christmas go by without seeing you," Tom said, his graying mustache spreading with his smile.

Ruby offered a strained, sickly smile in return. "Wish more people felt the same."

Tom nodded. "Never seen the place like this. Especially at Christmas."

"Picks up in the evening," Ruby said, playing right into the lie Tom had just told himself.

"Sure, sure," Tom agreed.

"Happy hour's still good."

"Right." His nod of agreement was a lie, too.

The place felt so sad, like a party had been thrown and no one had showed. It was no escape, offered no lift to his spirits.

No sense in rubbing it in, though. Tom decided to make it seem like his disappointment was all about his own situation. "Can't help but miss my girl at this time of year."

Ruby leaned forward, her white hair tumbling out of her bun, taking Tom's hand in her own.

He fought the urge to pull away. He didn't mind Ruby reaching out. He liked Ruby.

But it wasn't the right hand. It wasn't the right touch.

"Geena's coming home for Christmas, though, right?" Ruby asked. "You two have to celebrate her making it through her first semester. Bet she got straight 'A's, that one."

Tom took a breath, turning his face toward the window—and the sidewalk square bearing her name. "Not this year. Rob won't be coming home, you know. So she didn't see any reason…"

"Couldn't stand being here without him, you mean. She still has reason to be here," she assured him with a nod. "Don't you ever doubt that."

"Well. She did promise me New Year's," Tom said. "Besides, she's always had Christmas Eve with her mother. We had our own celebrations on another night—usually before Christmas. So, you know. I guess I should be used to not having her around. I mean, on the actual holiday."

Someone else was missing, of course—Tom and Ruby both knew that. Tom had grown to love another woman. He'd doubted, after his divorce, that it would ever happen again, but it had. And now, it was over. It had been over for quite some time. But this year, without the distraction of Geena, knowing he was going to be all alone in an empty house in the days leading up to Christmas, he was missing his love terribly. It stung like the loss was new all over again.

This year, Tom felt like part of him was gone.

Ruby nodded in a way that said she understood all too well how Tom was feeling. She leaned her slim body against the edge of the bar. Even then, when she was the age the world deemed, simply, *old*—the most dismissive term in the English language—she was lovely. Elegant. Every bit the graceful ballerina.

"Not sure what's worse," Ruby offered, glancing out at her nearly empty bar, "having already lost something you loved desperately or being in the process of losing it. Watching it ever so slowly slip out of your grasp. Both are agonizing in their own way."

Tom gulped down the rest of his drink instead of responding. He didn't want to get into some long philosophical discussion. Not about Geena's absence or his long-lost love.

"Merry Christmas, Ruby," he said, leaning in to kiss her cheek.

He gathered his coat and headed back out into the cold. Everything had changed. His life was different. And now, he knew that even Ruby's was different. He'd seen that with his own eyes.

He knew, with a pang in his heart, he'd probably never return to the old bar.

It was going to be a sad Christmas.

23.

2018

"**RUBY?**" Angela repeated.

Ruby pulled herself away from her reverie with a deep sigh.

"Where'd you go?" Angela asked. "What were you thinking about?"

"Oh, pfff," Elizabeth said with the toss of her hand. "Ruby's a sentimental sap. At her core, you'll find nothing but a pile of mush."

Angela laughed, relieved to find Elizabeth drifting back toward her usual good-natured tone. All around them, the bar continued to lighten, as the celebration of Tom grew increasingly louder, almost frenzied. Stories had given way to a sing-along around the piano—the entire crowd of regulars was engaged in a rather boisterous rendition of "One for My Baby."

But instead of teasing Elizabeth in return, Ruby frowned, looking toward the front window. "Who is that?" she asked. She had to shout it twice, so Angela could hear her over the out-of-tune singing.

Angela moved closer to the window to see where Ruby pointed. An older woman stood in the glow of the nearby streetlight, staring into the bar. Angela squinted, attempting to bring her into focus: short white hair, a heavy blue winter coat and matching scarf, drooping shoulders. Her hands had been stuffed into her coat pockets, and her expression was sour—sad, conflicted, concerned.

"Do you recognize her?" Ruby pressed.

"I'm—not sure, actually," Angela said.

"Seems awfully interested in this place," Ruby mused.

"Can she see us?" Elizabeth asked.

Angela wasn't sure about that, either. This time, though, she burst through the door, determined to find out.

24.

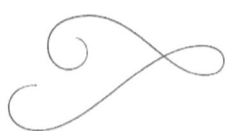

THE night air attacked Angela with its brutal chill. She crossed her arms over her bulky sweater, making a shield for her chest, wishing she had thought to grab her coat on the way out the door.

"Sorry," the woman said. "I shouldn't have been snooping around." Her cheeks were pink—but whether from cold or embarrassment, Angela couldn't tell.

"Oh, it's not snooping. More like a healthy dose of curiosity," Angela said, trying to make her voice sound light. "I know it looks a little rough through that window right now, but we're absolutely going to be open for Christmas."

"It's not that, it's…" The woman stopped, shook her head. She was crying.

Angela winced. "Are you all right, Ms.—"

"Cranston," she finished. "Helen."

"Helen," Angela repeated. "Are you sure you're all

right?" But the woman was staring so intently through the front window, Angela wondered if she'd even heard her.

"Helen?" Angela tried again. She followed her stare, finding Ruby standing directly on the opposite side of the glass.

Angela swallowed a gasp. Did Helen see Ruby? What did she think? Why was Ruby being so conspicuous?

Ruby waved. She pressed her nose against the glass. She knocked on the window.

Helen didn't wave back. She didn't shudder or point or even blink.

Ruby cocked her head to the side and glanced at Angela, motioning for her to come in.

Did she mean with Helen, though? Or did she want Angela to get rid of Helen?

Ruby pursed her lips in a semi-annoyed way, then pointed at Helen, pointed at Angela, and pointed at the door.

She couldn't be serious, could she? The whole place was teeming with spirits. Singing, shouting. Didn't Helen hear them? Angela could. Their voices were muffled, of course—but definitely audible from where she was standing.

"Did you ever steal something from someone?" Helen asked. "Something important?"

That did it. Angela was convinced that Helen had come here for a reason other than checking out the old bar. She had a story, something she needed to get off her chest.

"Helen, please," Angela said, reaching for the door. "Would you join me? It's cold out here. You look like you're freezing. I know I am."

"He used to come here, you know," Helen said, tilting her head upward to get a look at the vinyl reopening sign. "Didn't this place used to have a neon sign?" she asked, wrinkling her forehead. "Hard to picture what it looked like back then."

"He who? Please. Come inside and we'll talk about it," Angela promised. She placed one hand behind Helen's elbow and pointed with the other, urging her toward the entrance.

Helen's unexpected appearance inside Ruby's put an end to the singing, right in the middle of a rousing chorus of "Come Rain or Come Shine." The piano stopped. The drinking and storytelling stopped.

They all stared at Helen, waiting for some sign. Did she see them? Did she not?

"Haven't been inside this old place in years," Helen said, taking a few more tentative steps inside.

The regulars remained frozen in place. They'd turned themselves into statues.

Helen placed her hand on the back of a chair, currently occupied by Judy Woodward. She gripped the chair tighter and began to pull it backward.

Judy jumped to her feet and skittered out of the way.

"What was in here?" Helen asked, pointing at Judy's emptied glass.

"A—uh, a sidecar," Angela said, hoping she remembered right. Did Helen see the rest of the bottles and glasses scattered about? How would she explain it?

"Haven't heard of anyone drinking one of those in ages," Helen admitted, dropping into Judy's old seat. She sighed, staring into the glass. "Are you serving? Or…" She glanced about, at the ladders and buckets.

"No, no. I've just been practicing. Bartending is new to my résumé." She offered a nervous laugh, hoping to convince Helen.

Mrs. Cranston's nose turned a deeper shade of red as her eyes began to tear again.

"Helen?"

"I stole something precious."

"Stole what?" Angela watched as Ruby and Elizabeth, intent on hearing the old woman's confession, slipped into the empty chairs at their table.

Helen was absolutely beside herself; maybe even on the verge of a breakdown. She kept running her hands through her curly white hair—and her face was so twisted with agony that she seemed to be carving a deeper trench into each of her wrinkles.

"I was with him," she whispered, forcing her words out in a single gust of agony.

"Who?" Angela put her hand on Helen's back.

"Tom. When he died. He was with me."

"That's good, isn't it?" Angela tried. "He wasn't alone."

"I stole it from her," Helen said, shaking now.

Ruby covered her mouth with her fingers.

"His last moments," Helen said. "Those should have been Geena's. And I—I took them. Why did he send her away?"

"He sent her where, Helen?"

"Over to The Page Turner."

"He sent her—to The Page Turner?" Angela glanced across the table at Ruby and Elizabeth. They leaned forward, eyes wide, mouths slack, both paying rapt attention to Helen's story.

"I was supposed to sit with him while she was out," Helen confessed. "She was going to be gone a little while, she said. But there was a noise. Upstairs, you know? So I went and he was—he was on the floor. He wasn't breathing. But there was a note, I remember. On his nightstand."

"Did you see what it said?"

Helen tossed her hand. "It didn't make sense."

144

"Might help to talk about it, though," Angela said. Was that reasonable? Helpful? Or did it seem like she was being a busybody, as anxious for information as any other gossip-hungry resident? She wasn't sure. But Ruby nodded at her, indicating it was right to ask.

"'First love,'" Helen whispered. "That's what it said. Why would he write that?"

Elizabeth grew pale; Ruby lunged forward, grabbing Angela's wrist. "He was trying to get them together. Rob and Geena. It was his last wish."

"I shouldn't have been with him," Helen moaned. "I stole those minutes from her. I'd do anything to give them back."

"It's more important than ever to get Geena here. And Rob, too," Ruby insisted.

Elizabeth only stared.

"We should do something. For Tom. Hold a—a wake," Angela suggested.

"Pfff," Elizabeth muttered. "A wake. Why would you do that? With the Christmas holiday days away. Why would people want to come for a Christmas celebration at the same place where they'd just attended a funeral?"

"How is that any different than a church?" Ruby challenged.

But Helen, still oblivious to Ruby and Elizabeth, kept shaking her head. "He didn't—he refused any kind of funeral. He didn't want one."

"He was a regular," Ruby told Angela. "At one point, he used to be here all the time. Why do you think he was so nosy about what you were doing in here? Always coming by, working his way in with you, telling you stories, making you like him. Until you felt the need to show him around the place. Do you really think he needed a new Western to read every single week, or do you think that was an excuse to come down here, get another glimpse at what kind of progress you were making? Now's when we need to act, Angela. I can feel it. We have to do something. Get Rob and Geena out here. If not a wake, we should have a—what do you call it?"

"A celebration of life!" Angela blurted. "Surely, he wouldn't have had a problem with that. I bet everybody he worked with at the police department would come. And more—half of Sullivan would show up. He touched so many lives," she went on, thinking of the tales that only moments ago had been filling the old bar. "Let them all come and tell Tom stories and honor his memory."

"I don't know—" Helen moaned. "I can't—I just—"

"I'll level with you, Mrs. Cranston. Helen. I know about Geena's first love. You probably remember him, too."

"Sort of…He was that boy with long hair. What was his name…"

"Rob."

"That sounds familiar."

"Rob," Angela repeated. "Just like the name carved into the sidewalk outside that front door. 'Rob and Geena forever…'"

Helen cracked a smile. "Oh, I remember. Tom was so upset about that sidewalk back then."

"Think about it. Rob now owns The Page Turner. And Tom sent Geena out to buy a book!"

Helen's eyes swelled. "First love," she murmured.

"Tom's last wish was for Geena to reunite with Rob," Angela said, repeating Ruby's assumption. "I've already got Rob coming on opening night. But I know he's had Tom on his mind lately, and if we have a get-together in Tom's memory, I'm sure I can get him here for that, too. Think you could convince Geena?"

"I'll do it," Mrs. Cranston said, clearly finding solace in Angela's explanation. "I'll do it for Tom. And for Geena. It doesn't make up for taking her last few moments, but it's something."

25.

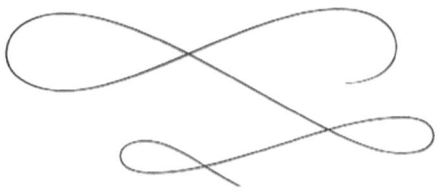

GEENA'S eyes blurred as she tried to read yet another student essay. Usually, grading final essays was delicious. She knew other professors at her university considered it something of a burden—it was understandable, really. At that point, so late in the semester, everyone was worn out. They were ready for a breather, not a stack of term papers that stretched from the floor to their knees.

But Geena considered it a reward. Here they were, four classes of students who were writing better, thinking more clearly, understanding what they read in a new way. It was the sign of time well spent. She had made her mark. Her students would go on to write better papers in whatever discipline they'd chosen to major in. Maybe go to grad school, like she did. Go on to teach their own classes and see proof, at the end of each semester, of their own time well spent.

She especially loved that last idea.

This semester, though, she was sitting at her childhood kitchen table. The house was uncomfortably still. Eerily quiet. It would never be *un*quiet. Her thoughts kept pinballing, making it hard to concentrate.

Her father was dead. It was still hard to wrap her brain around that fact. He wasn't gone for a week. He wasn't upstairs sleeping off a double shift. This was the beginning of a new life, a life minus her dad, the police officer and all-around tough guy who would take care of…well, anything, really. Without a second thought or grumble.

Here she was, alone, on the tightrope of life, without a net or a long pole for balance.

The funny thing was—if *funny* was even the right word—she hadn't realized how much she had still been depending on him. Here, well into her forties, a grown woman on her own. In the back of her mind, she had always known that he would be there *in case*. Should she have a legal problem or a boyfriend problem or even not get a teaching contract renewed. She could always come home—which was exactly what she'd done during one particularly disastrous semester at the height of the recession, claiming to be on "sabbatical" when the truth was that no one was hiring profs with her particular expertise. She'd stayed up in her old room, working morning to night, seeing no one but her father, writing new papers to submit to journals, snagging freelance editing jobs, and networking, networking—*constantly* networking, until finally landing a position in Vermont.

Her father had been there for her that fall. He would, she'd always known, be there for her again.

Until now.

The phone rang. Geena checked the clock on the computer, shocked to find that it was dinnertime. Her mother always called the house at dinnertime.

"Hey, Mom," she greeted.

"Geena," her mother said, sounding a little breathless. "How are you, dear?"

"I'm—fine. Lots of papers left, so—"

"You're still grading?"

"Yes, so I'd better—"

"You've never taken this long to grade final essays."

"Which is why I need to—"

"I'm flying up there."

"Oh, Mom, please. That's unnecessary. I—"

"Geena. You can't be comfortable all by yourself in your father's house."

"Why wouldn't I be?"

"Well, it's got to be—I mean, what kind of condition is the house in? If he wasn't in the best of health…"

Geena frowned; she supposed that curiosity never did die, not even when a relationship ended, especially if there had once been love. Geena got the feeling that her mother wanted to snoop, maybe every bit as much as she wanted to help her.

"You have a new house of your own to worry about," Geena reminded her. Her tax accountant husband had finally retired, moving her mother to Florida. "I do appreciate your offer, but I really don't need any more distractions, Mom. I can't do anything but finish grading. I'm under deadline. You and I would find a million things to do. Especially this time of year."

"Fine," her mother sighed. "But you'll need help afterward."

"Help?"

"With the house, of course. Emptying it out. Selling off the contents, putting it up for sale."

Geena flinched, realizing for the first time that this was, in fact, a possibility she needed to consider. She lived in Iowa. And then, when her teaching contract ran out next year, she might live in Arkansas or Georgia or Massachusetts. That was the life of a professor, wasn't it?

But sell off the house? Not yet. It didn't feel right. Mostly because somehow, it felt like her father should still be coming home any minute.

"Mom, I have to go. I'll talk to you later. Love you," Geena blurted, then hung up while her mother was still talking.

She wiped her eyes, freshened her coffee cup, and began to read the student paper pulled up on her computer.

Her eyes blurred all over again.

It's not like you don't have friends here, Geena scolded herself. People who, unlike her mother, had only good memories of her dad. People who could listen to her unload about how it felt like she had a canyon inside of her where her dad used to be. Of course she did.

Or did she? After all, she'd been gone a long time.

She supposed she could contact one of her friends in Iowa—but then again, maybe that was a bad idea, too. Those were work friends, the kind that accompanied her to department meetings. They didn't know her father—or, for that matter, anything personal about Geena. What they needed to know was that she could come back and teach next semester, and everything would be fine, fine.

Only, it wasn't.

Maybe if her dad had at least been open to a funeral. Some way for her to get some closure.

She pushed herself away from the table and climbed the stairs to her room. And before she quite knew why, she was in her closet, digging past the leftover old boots and sneakers and a few remnants of late-teenhood fads and the high school yearbooks. Until…there. She grinned to herself. There it was—the mangled shoebox—the one that had once contained her 1980s Reeboks. She curled her legs beneath her, pulling the box into her lap.

She managed a smile, remembering how she had chosen that particular box to hide all her Rob keepsakes. Her father would never even accidentally look inside an old Reebok box. And, in the beginning, her relationship with Rob had required some degree of secrecy. In the beginning, her father had considered him too rough for his only daughter. In the beginning, Rob was a constant source of bickering between them. Before Rob, her dad had often reminded her, there had been no slipping out late at night. No letting a boy in through her bedroom window. No cigarette stink in her clothes or the smell of beer on her breath. But then again, Geena had been quick to point out, there had also never been an offer from a boy to help her father work on the family car or provide a collector's copy of Tom's favorite author on his birthday.

She flipped the lid off to find the remnants of their time together still inside. A kind of first-love time capsule: concert tickets and a few dried roses and some silly carnival pictures. And senior prom pics. Geena in her permed hair and the red sequined Gunne Sax dress with the dyed-to-match shoes. She'd begged with everything she had for that too-expensive dress. Now it only looked ridiculous.

Rob looked dated, too, of course. Rob with his long hair and the Converse high-tops he wore with his tux. Wore with everything back then, actually. Even now, though, Rob still looked handsome in that picture. That crooked smile of his hadn't gone out of style.

Geena sifted through all the gifts Rob had given her—those cheap little trinkets kids bestow on their beloveds: plastic bracelets and mix-tapes and shells and barrettes for her hair. Pot metal rings. A half-used bottle of Wind Song cologne.

Rob had given her something else, though. Something that didn't fit in a box: His unwavering friendship. Above all else, Rob had been her friend. Maybe the best one she'd ever had.

She found herself aching for it now.

Somewhere in the confused aftermath of her father's death, it had finally come back to her that it had been Rob out there, on the sidewalk in front of The Page Turner. The middle-aged man who'd waved to her. Who had started to jog toward her. It was him.

He would have talked to her—wouldn't he? If her phone hadn't started to ring? If Mrs. Cranston hadn't begged Geena to come home as quickly as possible? If she hadn't run before acknowledging him?

These questions and more had found her in the shower and at the toaster and while she was brushing her teeth. She'd finally succumbed to the crush of her own curiosity, and had looked him up online.

She'd shuddered a bit when she'd learned that he actually owned The Page Turner. The same bookstore where they'd browsed the shelves together on Saturday afternoons, the way other couples browsed the aisles of the neighborhood video rental stores.

She'd nearly bumped her nose against her laptop screen trying to get a good look at his hands in the pictures he'd posted of himself, standing at the counter of The Page Turner. No ring. Which might not mean anything; after all, some guys didn't wear rings. Then again, it might also mean there would be no wife to annoy or anger if she were to get in touch, an old friend reaching out. Should she, though?

Sure, she still felt close to Rob. But did he remember things differently? He'd had a child—*Dad*, that was what the familiar-looking skateboarder had called out to him. That boy was now probably the same age Rob was when he and Geena'd gotten together. Did that color things differently? Did it make whatever they'd shared seem like nothing more than infatuation? Like kid stuff?

Did *he* ever think of them as being friends? Or was she some crummy ex, the kind you wind up telling yourself you're lucky to be rid of?

"Why didn't you ever tell me Rob bought the bookstore, Dad? And why were you so insistent I go out there?" she asked the shoebox—and her empty bedroom. "Did you finally change your mind about him? Or am I reading too much into this?"

The box provided no clear answer.

First love. Her dad had written that in a half-finished message on his nightstand.

"This is silly," she muttered, and started to return the cardboard lid. But she stopped when she caught sight of a familiar pointed metal tip.

She reached hesitantly into the box to remove the old nail attached to a cheap silver chain. Before she could second-guess herself, she fastened the clasp behind her neck.

In the months after Rob had given it to her, she'd practically lived in the old necklace. Worn it with every outfit, much to her father's dismay. When was the last time she had it on? Around the time of graduation? The first semester of college?

Geena tightened her fist around the nail as the answer came back to her.

26.

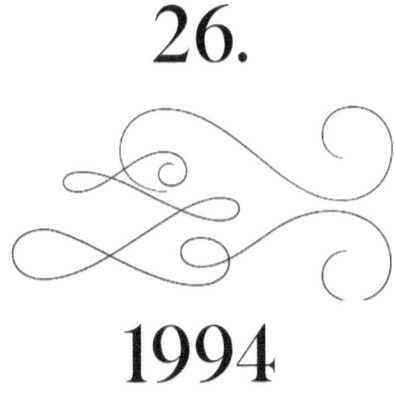

1994

GEENA put on her very best red maxi dress and distressed combat boots. A vintage black leather jacket purchased at Nellie's Fleas offered a perfect finishing touch. She stood in front of the old childhood bedroom mirror to examine her full fashion prowess.

Something was definitely wrong. She squinted, turning to the right and left. And grunted, realizing what it was.

Hurriedly, she plopped down on the edge of her bed and began to unlace the boots. She was in grad school now, and she didn't want to look like a kid.

Especially not today.

She pulled all her silver rings off, too, dropping them into her jewelry box. She tugged on her very adult-looking knee boots, draped a silk scarf around her neck, and slipped into her long black wool coat.

The necklace she'd originally chosen was still visible beneath the rolled hem of her silk scarf. Did she remove it? Leave it?

She wrapped her hand around the old nail on a chain. *Leave it*, she decided. She gave it a quick squeeze before hurrying out of the house.

As she raced toward Ruby's, it crossed her mind that the proper thing to do was bring a gift. It was Christmas, after all. But then again, maybe that seemed a little desperate. Or like overkill. Too much of an attempt to break the ice.

There'd been no letters, not for years. Geena had been the last to write. Over time, her thoughts on the matter had shifted incessantly, causing different questions to rise to the surface. Had he not received her letter? Had she written something that had made him mad? Had his feelings soured? Was he no longer interested? Was she unimportant? How could he think so little of her that he wouldn't even tell her straight-out one way or the other, just disappear and leave her to wonder? *Could* he write? Had something happened? Was he in a place that made writing impossible?

This last question brought her full-circle, to wonder, yet again, *Did he even receive my last letter?*

158

Geena'd run into his mother a couple of times, over at The Red Apple supermarket during her summer breaks. She always said hello, hoping Mrs. Hendrix would offer her some slice of information about Rob. But there had never been anything substantial, only the reassurance that he had not been injured or worse. The last time Geena saw her, Mrs. Hendrix had to be reminded of her name.

But now, though, *now*, Rob was home. Back from the service. And there would be a kind of Welcome Home party at Ruby's, thrown by a few friends. A late-afternoon informal get-together before happy hour.

Geena had not been invited specifically. But then again, no one in town had, either. The word had spread, as it always spread in Sullivan. *Come on by. Say hello to him. Welcome our hometown solider back.*

They even said it to her: "Sure Rob'd be glad to see you." That was from Sean Gibbs himself, his exact words as he gift-wrapped the shaving kit Geena'd bought for her father over at the men's specialty store.

Geena and Rob hadn't hung out with Sean Gibbs in high school. Back then, Sean had been more interested in his garage band. But now, he was telling her that he and "the guys" were bringing their acoustic guitars, and his sister was going to play piano. And while he was yammering on, Geena was thinking the whole time that if he'd arranged all that, he'd sure-ly been talking directly to Rob, which meant he knew for a fact that Rob wanted her to come. Rob had mentioned her. He had to have.

For the past week, Geena had thought of nothing else. Now, she couldn't get there fast enough. Ruby's would be the perfect place to see him again—surrounded by a hundred of Sullivan's rowdiest, who would all help cover her awkwardness. And there would surely be initial awkwardness, but not for long. Not with Rob.

Her heart was beating dangerously fast and her mouth was burning and her palms were sweating and all the butterflies that had ever been in her stomach were alive and well. After the world's longest pause, she and Rob were mere moments away from picking up where their conversation had left off.

Her tires squealed a bit as she pulled into a parking space. She broke into a sprint down the sidewalk, pausing only once to greet a couple she had graduated with.

She put her hand on the door, then pulled it away. Not yet. She couldn't just go barreling in there. She needed a peek. The tiniest little glimpse. To prepare herself.

She put her face against the window. Sure enough, Sean was inside, sitting on a stool and plucking a guitar. Geena's eyes drifted past a few vaguely familiar faces—former classmates, old neighbors. There he was! Rob. She smiled, her eyes tearing. She'd never seen him without his long hair. And he was beefy—far more muscular than she remembered. He wore a black sweater and jeans, like he might have worn five or six years ago. And his tried-and-true Converse.

Slowly, though, Geena's smile faded. And it began to sink in that the closely cropped hair and the muscular frame weren't the only things that had changed. Even from that distance, she could tell—that wasn't the same carefree, wild Rob.

But then again, why would he be? He'd been halfway across the world. He had been witness to events Geena had only seen described in headlines. He held himself with a different confidence—a more worldly, more self-assured version of the Rob that Geena had known, the one with that crummy Caprice and the bad boy reputation.

In the meantime, Geena had been to college. She had graduated. It seemed so ordinary, suddenly. She had never stopped being a schoolgirl. In grad school, sure. But a classroom was still protection, wasn't it? It wasn't "the real world."

She stared, feeling like a spy, unable to pry her eyes away. A woman—attractive, dark-headed—approached Rob, smiling. She leaned in, kissed his cheek. Rob wrapped an arm around her, hugged her back.

Geena flinched, pulled away from the window. Her

head was a tornado.

She felt ridiculous suddenly, wearing the nail necklace and arriving with all that silly hope in her heart. After all, if Rob had wanted to see her, he would have called the house. Wouldn't he? She'd been home for a week. Sean Gibbs had seen her. Surely he would have told Rob.

What a numbskull she was.

Rob's life had rolled forward. At this point, she was nothing more than a girl he used to know.

She pressed her back against the wall, trying to catch her breath.

The door flew open, and Geena grabbed the lapel of her coat, squishing it together, covering up the nail on the chain.

She started breathing again when a man's face emerged beneath a mop of gray hair. "Hey, Geena," he greeted.

"Dr. Porter." Geena smiled at her old high school principal.

"Grad school treating you well?"

Geena nodded as her eyes found it again, only a few feet from where they were standing: that stupid sidewalk square. Had it become a joke? Had Rob laughed about it with the woman inside? Had he told her about the foolish kids they'd been? *4Ever*. How embarrassing. Her father had told her, angrily, that it would be someday. He was so right. Why hadn't she listened?

"Good, good," Dr. Porter said in a kind of offhanded, slightly disinterested tone. He paused, waiting for her to say something back—ask how the old school was, make some comment about the football team, something. She couldn't. Small talk was digging knives into her.

She couldn't look Dr. Porter in the face, either. Here she was, former valedictorian, behaving like the dope of the world. How dumb she'd been, imagining that time had somehow stopped for Rob, that she'd find him the same, having done nothing but sit around waiting for her return, the prodigal girlfriend.

"I have to warn you, it won't be the same," Dr. Porter said, pointing toward the bar.

Geena felt the blood rush out of her head. He knew. Everyone knew. Here he was, trying to warn her.

"I—sorry?" Geena muttered.

"The bar. Ruby's Place. It's not the same. Owner passed away some time ago, and her family's been trying to run it."

"Oh." Relief poured across her shoulders.

"Isn't the same without old Ruby," Dr. Porter said. "In fact, there's talk the place might shut down completely. Odd. Can't imagine Sullivan without Ruby's Place." He shook his head.

"Well," he finally announced, reaching for the door to let her in. "I won't keep you. I'm sure Rob—"

Geena lunged forward, placed a hand on his arm to stop him. "Wait!" she shouted.

Dr. Porter took a step away from the door, frowning at her. "Something wrong?"

"No, I—you know, I left my wallet in the car. I should—" She gestured somewhere behind her shoulder, backed up, and hurried down the sidewalk.

She jumped behind the wheel and took off, racing home, where she quickly changed back into her jeans, dropped the nail on a chain back into the old Reebok shoebox, and shoved it into the darkest corner of her closet, never to be taken out again.

27.

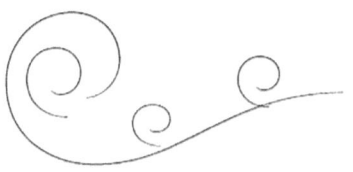

2018

"DIDN'T throw it away, though," Geena reminded herself, still staring into the box in her lap. "That has to mean something." She'd never mentioned going to Ruby's or seeing Rob to her dad, though. He'd asked that night, over dinner. But she'd shrugged. "I thought about it, but decided not to go. Went out to do a little holiday shopping instead."

She'd topped up her dad's iced tea glass, attempting to distract him. Afraid he could see through her lie. She'd hummed as she'd scooped more green beans onto her plate, pretending to be ravenous. Even then, she'd doubted she'd fooled him.

She couldn't fool herself, either. It was a disorienting thing, mourning the loss of someone who had already been gone for years. She was sure her dad could see the shock and searing ache on her face.

Now, a lifetime later, Geena touched the nail hanging around her neck. "Why, Dad?" she asked again. "Why'd you send me to The Page Turner?"

The only response she received was the ringing of the doorbell.

Geena put the lid back on the box and left it on the floor. She raced downstairs, dropping the nail on the chain inside her bulky sweater along the way, though she wasn't sure why she felt the need to hide it.

She was panting by the time she threw the door open.

"Mrs. Cranston," she said, surprised by the woman's appearance. The neighbor had already been by—just yesterday—and had called four times—and delivered three casseroles. She'd already paid her respects.

Mrs. Cranston raised a brown paper shopping bag. "Gingerbread cookies," she announced.

Geena accepted the bag, cradling it in her arms. But when she glanced inside, she didn't see finished cookies—only the ingredients. Geena smiled at her over the top of the bag. Even Mrs. Cranston remembered the summer her parents divorced, and how Geena had padded barefoot to her house every morning. Remembered how she'd helped make Geena forget all her problems for a couple of hours each morning while the two of them sifted flour and folded new ingredients into a batter.

She hadn't baked much in the past few years. But maybe, just maybe, this was what she needed.

"You're not going to let me do this on my own, are you?" Geena joked. "I have to admit, I'm rusty."

Mrs. Cranston smiled; this is what she'd wanted, it seemed—to come inside, to help Geena. This was her true sympathy card, delivered by hand, in person.

"It's the nicest gesture anyone's extended since Dad's passing," Geena said as the women walked into the kitchen. And she meant it.

They set to work, digging through Tom's cabinets for bowls big enough to hold all their ingredients.

"You know," Mrs. Cranston said offhandedly, "I saw Angela today. She's the new owner of Ruby's Place."

"Yeah?" Geena asked, as a stick of butter began to melt in a pot on the stove's front burner. She didn't really want to press for more information. In fact, the mere mention of Ruby's gave her a queasy feeling. That awful sidewalk in front of the bar was where her father'd had his heart attack. Where she'd seen Rob. Where her name was still carved into cement. Where words between them had gone unsaid and where she'd been standing when Mrs. Cranston had called, begging her to hurry.

Suddenly, that area seemed to be the convergence of everything unfinished or unsatisfying or just plain sad in Geena's life.

But Mrs. Cranston appeared to have no intention of dropping the subject. Watching anxiously for Geena's reaction, she continued, "Angela suggested having a celebration of life there."

"For—what? For Dad?" Geena pulled her hand away from the pot, her spoon dripping melted butter onto the floor.

"Your dad was awfully fond of the place," Mrs. Cranston said.

"Not Ruby's. Dad never went there."

"Oh, yes. He did. He and his—well. You know."

Geena shook her head. "His what?"

Mrs. Cranston's face flamed like a burner cranked all the way up. "Oh," she said, placing a hand on her chest. "Never mind."

"Never mind what?" Geena pressed.

"He never told you? Not—not ever?"

"Tell me *what?*"

Mrs. Cranston sighed. "He may not have wanted you to know," she said shyly.

"Mrs. Cranston!"

She wiped her hands and took a deep breath, as though having to work up to the news. "He had a—well. A woman friend."

"What are you talking about?"

"After your mother. When you were young. He—"

"He had a *girlfriend*?"

Mrs. Cranston shrugged, still squirming against the guilt of betraying what had apparently been a confidence. "I thought he would have told you. After so long, I didn't think it would still be a secret."

Geena's head swirled. "How could this gossipy town have kept it from me? Why would I have never heard about it from anyone?"

"I suppose secrets travel in circles. Young people are simply more concerned with the gossip in their own circle."

Mrs. Cranston returned to mixing ingredients. Geena put her spoon back in the pot. The butter was about to brown, but her head was spinning too turbulently for her to realize she needed to lift it off the burner.

"I just thought—" Mrs. Cranston blubbered. She was crying, Geena noted with surprise. Had she hurt Mrs. Cranston's feelings somehow? She hadn't meant to. "I really wanted to do this for him," Mrs. Cranston continued. "And you. Your family was so kind after my husband passed—could always lean on Tom—so special..."

Geena reached out to console Mrs. Cranston. It was

normal to be upset when someone died. Geena was upset. She'd been crying herself to sleep. She had burst into tears flipping through the channels and bumping into an old Western on late-night TV. But was Mrs. Cranston more upset than a neighbor should have been?

Geena's eyes swelled as she continued to stare at Mrs. Cranston, the woman who had been so nice to her when she was little. The woman who had always lived next door to her father.

The woman who was about the same age as her father.

And knew about another woman?

Was it possible? Her father—and Mrs. Cranston?

"I—I think a celebration of life for him at Ruby's would be lovely."

"Yes! Yes it would!" Mrs. Cranston exclaimed, pulling some Kleenex from her cardigan pocket. "Oh, Geena, I'm so glad you like the idea." She threw her arms around Geena's neck and hugged her tightly.

Geena's arms were a bit limper in response. She had a lot to process.

The only thing she was absolutely sure of was that she was even more anxious than ever to talk to someone who would understand how she felt. Someone who had known her father. Someone who would sit quietly and make no assumptions.

Someone like Rob.

28.

KELLY Chastain burst through the door at closing time, waving the quickest of goodbyes to Rob, her boss. The way she'd been bolting from The Page Turner each evening, she probably had Rob thinking she couldn't wait to be rid of him. But the truth was, she had a workout to get to. And the quicker she got to the gym, the quicker the whole half-hour torture session would be over with.

She hadn't told Rob, though. It felt like admitting to your boss you had a full-on drinking problem you were trying to kick. Maybe fruitcake or Christmas-tree-shaped donuts weren't going to mess with her brain the same way, make her start shelving books in the wrong order and slurring inappropriate comments at customers. But as far as Kelly was concerned, any weakness needed to be concealed from an employer—even a kind one. Even one she adored. Even Rob.

She drove to the Y, where she and her husband were

shelling out fifty-nine bucks a month for a senior couple membership—not that her husband had even once accompanied her to any class. Not water aerobics or weight lifting. He hadn't tried pickleball, either, even though Kelly had assured him it was easy to learn and the leagues at the Y were populated by white-hairs just like them.

It was too bad, really. A little activity would have done his old-man gut some good. Mostly, having him in the building would have made her feel a little less on her own, and that would have been doing *her* some good.

Kelly changed into her sweat pants and New Balances, slammed the locker door, and pinned the key to her waistband as a new song came on the sound system. Kelly had decided that the most cruel joke in the world was having to listen to Christmas music at the gym. It played in the bathrooms. It played on the staircases. It played in the basketball courts and the pool. It blared through spin classes.

It was driving her nuts. When she wasn't even allowed nuts, especially not walnuts covered in dark chocolate. All that music was doing was reminding her of the goodies she was currently not consuming.

She grabbed her towel and trudged upstairs. She was at the hard part of her turning-over-a-new-leaf plan. At this point, her idea was no longer shiny and exciting. Her muscles were sore and she was tired and it seemed like everywhere she went, all around her people were eating sugar cookies, and she was literally dreaming every night of delectably sweet and calorie-laden venti peppermint lattes.

At her age—sixty-seven, but who was counting anymore?—every ounce of weight she put on hardened into concrete. This year, she'd promised, she was not going to join her husband in his-and-hers turkey comas. She was not going to make two pies, pecan for him and pumpkin for her. She was going to be reasonable. Couldn't a woman still enjoy herself and not go hog-wild?

Still. The old Kelly—the one that had always gorged herself during the Christmas season—wanted the latte and the turkey dressing. She wanted an apricot cake with toasted coconut topping, the one they made over at Sampson's Bakery. The whole dang thing. By herself.

Wasn't that what the holidays were about? Wasn't it a time for gaudiness and flat-up gluttony, the more the better? Not just one string of lights around the front yard but fifty. Not just a few tasteful ornaments, but a whole attic full. Not just one candy, but the whole box. The holidays were all about overdoing it: overindulgence, overspending, overeating.

Moderation, Kelly, she reminded herself. But at this time of year, moderation felt like punishment, like she wasn't even having Christmas at all.

"Hey, there, Kel," Colby said with a smile. As the Y's afternoon personal trainer and building maintainer, a full forty-plus years her junior, Colby had made it a point to be nice to her, the dumpy old lady who came in every single day at the exact hour when most people had fled the place for dinner.

Kelly figured if she exercised right before supper—traditionally her biggest meal of the day—she would kill her appetite. Who wanted a giant plate of fried chicken and an apple pie after spending a solid half hour on the treadmill?

Exhaustion—the new South Beach Diet.

Colby hummed along to "Silver Bells" as he disinfected the hand grips on the elliptical trainers and stationary bikes.

Kelly stepped onto a treadmill and punched the buttons, trying desperately to remember how she got to her favorite program.

Colby reached over her shoulder, hit the combination that activated a pattern of flashing lights. The belt on her treadmill began to whir into action.

Kelly hurriedly started moving her feet, embarrassed that it was part of Colby's afternoon duties to get her treadmill to work. He even had the codes for her favorite workouts memorized.

"So you probably got a story, right?" Colby asked, smiling at her as he wiped down the treadmill next to her.

What did that mean? Was he insinuating that surely she had to be more interesting than this? Some old lady at the gym at dinnertime, hiding out from chocolate pretzels and peanut butter fudge. Was that it?

"About Tom?" Colby pressed. "Tom Barister?"

"Why would I have a story about Tom?"

"Everybody does, right?"

"Do you mean—are you talking about me being at work over at The Page Turner when he had his heart attack?"

"And then the—what'd they call it?"

"Sudden cardiac arrest. I heard. It's all over town. Poor Geena."

"Yeah, but you heard the rest, too, right?"

"What rest?" Kelly was already starting to pant.

"They're going to have a celebration of his life. A party in his honor. At Ruby's Place."

"They are? The place isn't even open yet."

"Yeah. But they decided to hold it there, anyway. Before the grand opening. With Geena's okay. Couldn't do anything like that without her blessing. But yeah, Angela's hosting it."

"Huh." Slowly, the news began to filter into the deepest levels of Kelly's brain.

"So do you have a story? About Tom? I mean, everybody in this town seems to. That's the point of the celebration, right? To share stories about him. Do you have one?"

"I—" Kelly's head spun back to the bookstore. And to her employer. The kind one who'd dug a definite soft spot inside of her. "I bet I know someone who does."

29.

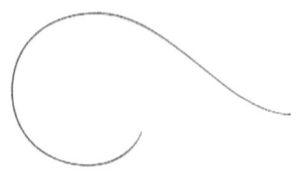

THAT Saturday, Rob pulled into his usual parking space to find Justin already waiting for him outside the entrance of The Page Turner. Casually leaning against the entrance, foot propped on his skateboard.

"What's up?" Rob called, pulling himself from the cab of his truck and trying, desperately, to keep fear out of his voice. It was odd for Justin to be here so early on a Saturday. What Rob's mother said when Justin was born had turned out to be true: *Little kids, little problems. Big kids, big problems.* Or, if not really problems, certainly bigger worries. Justin was a good kid—in by curfew, solid "B" average. But he was still a kid. And this whole girlfriend thing…

Back in high school, given the opportunity, Rob would have done the craziest, most reckless thing to be with Geena. Jumped off the edge of the world if she'd held out her hand and asked him to.

178

And now…

Why was Justin here, exactly?

Justin shrugged inside his coat—a kind of *bet you didn't expect to see me* hello. "I thought—couple extra hours at the store."

"So you're looking for some cash?"

"And maybe the truck?"

Rob laughed. "Only if you tell me about her, already. And give me the scoop on what you're planning for tonight."

"Daaaaaad."

"No way, man. No way am I going to hand over my keys and my cash without a little information. If not a full-on confession."

Justin moaned, throwing his head back.

"What's her name?"

"Sarah. Okay? Happy now?"

"Well," Rob said, wrapping his arm around Justin's neck and drawing him close, "it's a start."

"You're going to hold this thing over my head all day, aren't you?"

"Probably." Rob squinted at the front door, which was covered in multi-colored Post-its.

"And you're not going to pay me or give me the keys until I spill my guts."

"You know me all too well," he said, slightly distracted now as he began to read the messages. All were from Angela, and all were saying the same basic thing: "Stopped by, need to talk." "Come by Ruby's when you get in." "Something I need to talk to you about."

"Don't think I won't remember this," Justin teased as Rob tugged the Post-its down and fed his key into the door. "Don't think that one day, when the tables are turned, I'm not going to string you along, dangle some carrot in front of your nose."

"Uh-huh." Rob shoved the Post-its into his pocket.

"And I will *relish* it," Justin went on as the two stepped inside.

"I'd expect nothing less, son," Rob said, flipping the "Open" sign to face the street.

Justin shucked his coat. "All right. Where do I start?"

"Inventory," Rob barked, pointing at a row of boxes on the floor. He booted his computer, wondering what was so incredibly important across the street. Maybe he needed to go over there first thing.

"More movers?" Justin asked.

"Nah. Got a woman in the other day who decided to get rid of a bunch of stuff to make room for her Christmas tree—sounded like some gargantuan fake thing." He cringed.

"Whatever powers your sled, right?" Justin grabbed the box and propped it on the counter.

"This girl must be pretty special if you jump into inventory without a single protest," Rob observed. "You hate inventory more than I do, I think."

"I reserve the right to refuse comment at this time," Justin declared, sending Rob into a round of deep laughter. He loved that kid. He loved that he could tease him. He loved that he knew Justin was well aware that the dad in him would, in the end, hand over the keys and cash no matter what. He loved that this was all a game they were playing so that Justin could finally come clean about his girl, this Sarah.

"Listen," Rob said, "I have to go across the street for a second. Think you can hold down the fort?"

Before he was out from behind the front counter, the door flew open, and Kelly arrived in a *whoosh*—all pink from the cold.

"Got us some help today," Rob said, pointing at Justin.

"Hey, Kelly," Justin called out.

Kelly nodded. She had an about-to-explode-with-news look as she tugged furiously at her scarf. As if that scarf was somehow holding her secret inside.

"Everything okay?" Rob asked.

"Well," she said, finally freeing herself and draping the

scarf on the coat rack beside the door, "I heard something at the gym you might be interested in." Kelly worked her jaw a bit, like this thing she was about to tell them was so monumental, she needed to warm up her muscles to spit it out.

"Heard something in this town?" Justin grumbled. "Shocking."

Rob nudged him. "Whadja hear?" he asked Kelly.

Kelly's face was sober. Serious. "It's about Tom. Angela's hosting a celebration of his life over at the bar."

"She is? She left all kinds of messages on the door. Wonder if she needs some help with it. When's it scheduled?"

"Soon. Day after tomorrow."

"Day after—?"

"They wanted to have it quickly. Everyone felt the need to do something—you know, he said he wanted no funeral. But he made such a lasting mark on so many. They all wanted to share their stories. And everyone wanted to make sure to have it before the big Christmas Eve opening."

"By 'everyone,' you actually mean—"

"Geena," Kelly finished. "She okayed it, of course."

Rob nodded.

"You going, Dad?" Justin asked, his voice chipper.

"I dunno. Have to think about it. Maybe."

"Surely you have quite a few stories," Kelly sang, obviously trying to coax him away from his hesitation.

"Why's that?" Justin asked. "Wasn't that guy a police officer? I think Sarah's older sister said he was. Did you get *arrested*, Dad?" he teased.

But Rob wasn't laughing anymore. He was clearly done playing around. "No," he said abruptly. "I didn't."

Justin looked suddenly horrified. "What? What'd I say?"

Kelly shrugged. "Nothing." Her eyes registered an apology for dropping quite the bomb on Rob in front of his son.

"Aw, no." Justin slammed a book down on the counter. "Nothing in this town is literally *nothing*. Anytime somebody goes slinging that word around, it means it's definitely something. What's the deal?"

But Rob didn't feel like discussing anything right then. Even though he knew it was Justin's attempt to get back to a normal-sounding conversation. "Forget it. Not important," he told his son, then leaned over the counter to point at a metal cart. "Filled that one up for you last night," he told Kelly. "Ready to be shelved."

"If Angela left you notes on the door, she probably needs to see you quickly…" Kelly reminded him.

Rob nodded. "Yeah. Yeah, I should go," he started. But now that he knew what she wanted to talk to him about involved the Barister family, he felt himself dragging his feet.

Luckily, the bell on the door rang and a woman walked in shaking the snow from her hair. Rob regained his composure enough to ask her if it was getting bad out. She mouthed a polite "Burr!" in response, complete with a shiver, before saying she was looking for a present for her niece and did they have anything for a twelve-year-old book addict? Rob scurried to lead her down the right aisle and away from Justin's quizzical stare.

He showed her the classics—some of his illustrated editions of *The Secret Garden* and a leather-bound *Little Women*. Both were guaranteed to "make your niece feel grown-up," he assured her. As she carried the books to the counter, Rob hid out in the Poetry section. Pretended to be gathering up his tools from a display table he'd fixed the day before—a pesky wobbling leg that had been sending every propped-up book tumbling onto the floor.

He gripped his hammer and the small cup of nails. And before he could stop himself, there he went again, his thoughts going straight back to a long-gone Christmas, the last he'd spent with Geena, when he'd given her a nail on a chain. He felt it all over again—how emotional the whole thing had been, a mix of love and fear and hope. How he had wished on every one of the stars visible through the windshield of his Chevy for what they had to go on forever.

It'd been so different with the girl he'd actually married, with Maria. She'd chased him during something of a low point. He'd felt strangely raw and exposed just out of the service. Besides, he'd never been pursued before—not like that. It had flattered him. He'd liked not being the one doing the work— all that convincing, the planning.

Had he chosen something because it was easy? Maybe. In the beginning, at least. But there'd been affection, too, even in the midst of several rough patches, all their getting together and breaking up—at least, until Maria issued the ultimatum he figured was coming. Either they were all in or all out.

They'd plunged, even though Rob wasn't entirely sure. Maria was lovely, he'd told himself. And after all their ups and downs, they'd stuck it out. Didn't that predict success? How could they go wrong?

They had, though. So wrong, in fact, that Maria became something of a taste he'd developed an aversion to. The sound of her voice could make his stomach churn. Judging by the looks she shot him, she'd developed a similar distaste.

There had been no aversion to Geena, though. It had all been good, and then it suddenly didn't exist anymore.

Almost like…

Well. That was sort of how it was when someone died,

wasn't it?

It had certainly been that way with Tom. He'd been in Rob's store the day of his heart attack, picking up some new reads. They'd chatted like always, Tom telling new stories, Rob laughing with him. And now—simply gone.

Rob had kicked himself a hundred times for not visiting Tom, not taking him a new L'Amour and telling him how much he missed him at the store. He kicked himself for not acting like a friend. There was no going to visit him now. No do-overs. No second shots.

Geena's not dead, though. She's here in Sullivan. And she'll be at her dad's remembrance. The words coursed through him, singeing his nerves along the way.

Rob could talk to her there. Explain how badly he felt for not coming to see Tom. Tell her that her dad had left a hole, and how he knew it was nothing compared to how she felt. Being there for her was the right thing to do. No matter what the hell had happened between the two of them. Even now, he wasn't sure what word to tack to it. Fizzle? Spoil? Cool?

It didn't matter.

Maybe he and Geena weren't a couple anymore, but the way she could infiltrate his thoughts proved she was still important. When someone was important, you didn't shrug them off. You behaved honorably. You made sure they knew they could count on you.

Rob raced back out of the Poetry aisles, out the door, and across the street.

He knocked on Ruby's green door. When no one answered immediately, he knocked again, louder. He knocked incessantly, practically bloodying his knuckles.

When Angela appeared in the doorway, he announced, "I got your messages. I'll do anything I can to help with the party in Tom's memory."

30.

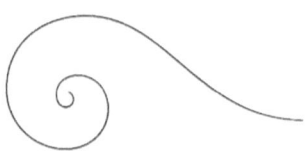

SCOTT Drummond pulled his Ford EcoSport into the gas station two blocks from home. Despite its immaculate appearance on the outside—always freshly waxed, free of nicks or dings or even so much as a spec of rust—inside, it was a sloppy mess. The floorboards were chronically crammed full of gym bags and one of his sons' Nerf guns and tiny toy cars and random broken pencils and crayons. His daughter's last spelling test had been taped to the glove compartment, where she would be sure he would see it reaching for the garage door opener each and every night.

Alessandra was a terrible speller. Horrendous. The kind of bad that had made him wish he and his wife hadn't given her a first name with so many letters in it. (*Ann*, he'd often thought. *What was wrong with Ann?*) So the perfect score on the spelling test was a big deal. Oscar-level. At least, it was in the Drummond world.

The car smelled strange, too. Like mud and hamburgers with onions and old shoes. In fact, one of his sons had been screaming, earlier that very morning, about a lost sneaker. And judging by the stench invading his nose, it was probably wedged under one of his seats.

He'd look later. He was tired and he needed to get to work.

Besides, once his kids had come along, he'd officially given up on the idea of anything he owned ever appearing completely in order again. At least he still had his office at the bank, with its tidy inboxes and outboxes, the wastebasket emptied each night, the houseplant on the top filing cabinet that he trimmed religiously, making sure it was never overgrown.

Everything else in his life pretty much looked like it had been hit by a bomb.

He popped the door, reached for a nozzle, fed it into the tank. It was cold that morning. Really cold. Bitter. That was a better word.

He grunted as he squeezed the pump, watching the numbers whiz by. He was good with numbers. No—he *liked* numbers, that was more accurate. He had always liked them. He liked their order and their certainty and their inability to change. A four was always a four. It behaved forever like a four. You could always count on four to do its job.

Children, though…They were more like blobs in a lava lamp, always shifting and morphing and turning into something else right when you thought you had a handle on them. Billy the soccer player suddenly wants to play the flute. Alessandra loves ballet until she breaks into tears as he drives her out to her lessons, accusing him of torturing her. Friends came and went with the frequency of a slamming screen door in the summer. All the coming and goings, the bare feet and ear infections, the screaming and the wet jackets slung on the staircase…

"Excuse me," a voice rang out. Scott jumped out of his own thoughts and found a familiar face smiling at him, waving a windshield squeegee—the ones that always waited around in buckets of solution near the gas pumps.

"Thought you might want this," Mrs. Cohen offered. "I know how you like a clean windshield."

Scott chuckled to himself. No one had offered him one of those squeegees in ages. Fifteen years ago, he'd been quite the small-town eligible bachelor. Women had brought him squeegees at the gas station and cupcakes at the bank, and when he'd shown up alone to the movie theater for a Sunday matinee (once one of his favorite pastimes), the single concessions worker had waved her fingers at him and said, "On me" with a wink.

"Thank you," Scott said, sliding the squeegee out of Mrs. Cohen's hand. "If anyone would remember me and windshields, it'd be you," he observed.

"Well, you did score the highest of all my driver's ed students," Mrs. Cohen agreed.

They shared a foggy-eyed laugh, their nods signaling an acknowledgment of how odd it was that time could fly by so quickly.

"Big plans for the holiday?" Mrs. Cohen called out, pulling some trash from her backseat and tossing it into a nearby wastebasket.

"I'm not sure yet," Scott said. In truth, his wife had made reservations at a Colorado ski resort months ago. But there was something about it—he kept trying to reassure himself maybe they wouldn't go after all.

Christmas wasn't really Christmas if he wasn't in Sullivan. Tradition wasn't about being in a new, unrecognizable place. It was decorating the same old tree, shopping the same old toy aisles, singing the same old carols with his wife while they sat on the floor of the same old living room assembling the current lot of toys for "Santa" to deliver on Christmas morning.

"Sure remember how you and your dad always spent Christmas at Ruby's Place," Mrs. Cohen remarked.

Scott came to an abrupt halt cleaning his windshield.

"You and Walter, both of you dressed to impress," Mrs. Cohen went on. "I remember one year—you were, I don't know, six maybe. In your three-piece suit, with a boutonnière. Sure were a sight."

Scott glanced down at his hazy reflection in the windshield. He had grown old enough to look like his father. Staring at his own reflection made Scott see, in his mind's eye, Walter coaching his Little League team, taking him fishing on summer weekends, or daring him ("but don't tell your mother") to sled down Sullivan's tallest hill—the one out by the defunct driving range.

It never did get easier, not having him around for Christmas. Scott hadn't seen his dad in—he always had to stop to count it up again—twenty-six years. It occurred to him that he was getting to the tipping point of being without his dad more years than he'd been with him. Maybe that had something to do with why the Colorado vacation was bothering him so much.

"Think Angela's going to get it open?" Mrs. Cohen shouted.

"Come again?"

"Ruby's Place. You think she's going to get it open?"

"Oh. I wouldn't have any idea."

"You handled the loan, though, didn't you? At the

bank?"

"And the payments have been coming in as regular as Sunday morning," Scott offered. "But as far as Angela's time-line…"

Mrs. Cohen nodded.

"Angela grew up at Ruby's, same as me," Scott reassured her. "You won't find anybody who loves that place or wants to do right by it more than she does." He found himself smiling saying it.

Mrs. Cohen had fallen silent.

"Do you have plans of your own—" he started, but Mrs. Cohen had her back to him, shoving her credit card into her billfold. She lurched behind her front seat and started her car.

He shook his head at himself as he returned the squee-gee. Of course she hadn't been flirting with him. Nobody did that anymore. And she wasn't remembering times gone by, ei-ther. Wasn't even really all that interested in catching up with him. She'd simply been fishing for information.

"Gossip," he muttered, cutting off the nozzle and slid-ing behind the steering wheel.

He wiggled his nose as he started the engine. Boy, did his car stink.

DOWNTOWN, Scott's Ford puttered to a stop in front of the Bank of Sullivan. He pulled himself out, reached beneath the driver's seat, and patted the floorboards until his fingertips bumped into a leathery foreign object. He heaved and hoed and heaved again, and when the shoe finally popped free, he staggered backward a few feet.

"Ha," he said, smiling at the sneaker. "Knew you were in there."

He popped the trunk and dropped the shoe inside. "Better you stink in there," he grumbled. He'd buy his son a new pair during lunch. Throw the old ones away at home. He couldn't toss them in a public trash can. No one should have to endure that smell.

Down the block, voices called out to each other. He glanced up, finding Rob hurrying across the street, out of his bookstore and toward the old bar. A woman shouted something back at him. It had to be Angela—he'd recognized her the day she'd first approached him at the bank for a loan, and he recognized her now, even from that distance, by that crazy brown hat she wore everywhere. Sure wasn't anything like the fancy dresses she'd worn to Christmas Eves at Ruby's when they were kids.

He thought of Mrs. Cohen, and he started to call out to her.

But he stopped himself, and watched her usher Rob into the bar instead.

Whatever she was up to in there, he told himself, it really wasn't any of his business.

His eye landed on that enormous vinyl sign, though—"Opening Christmas Eve!"—and his fingers found the cell phone in his pocket. He dialed home. When his wife answered, he asked, "Just how final are those reservations of ours?"

31.

"THAT kid's stopped in the street to stare into this place twice today," Ruby said, propping her hands on her hips.

"What kid?" Angela asked, rattling the ice in her cocktail shaker. She didn't see any kids, only Scott peering into the window. After a moment, his chest puffed out with a deep breath and he turned away, disappearing down the sidewalk. Angela poured the contents of her blender—a margarita—into a glass and pushed it across the bar, toward Barbara Lewis.

"Mine," Walter said, clunking his scotch glass on the bar. "Although, he's not a kid anymore."

"He's thinking of you," Ruby said. "Maybe he'll come for the grand opening."

"He has another life," Walter assured her. "Other plans."

"How do you know?" Angela asked.

"I know," he sighed.

"I could talk to him for you," Angela offered. "I'm at the bank all the time, I—"

"No, don't," Walter insisted. He added, in a tone that said he didn't want to discuss it anymore, "Everyone deserves their own life."

Angela refilled his scotch, but Walter had already turned away.

"Hey, Wa—" Angela started, raising the glass.

Walter refused to answer, shuffling across the bar, snaking through all the tables that Angela had carefully arranged.

Sadly, she lowered the glass again. She hadn't meant to upset him.

Ruby offered Angela a grin and a shrug, nodding at her in understanding. She hadn't meant to upset him, either.

"I'm glad you're doing this for Tom," Ruby told Angela, changing the subject.

"Yeah, I hope no one minds the whole work-in-progress feel," Angela admitted.

"Hardly a work-in-progress feel left," Elizabeth announced from her stool. For that evening's happy hour, she'd chosen to wear a long burgundy dress with a black and white silk scarf draped at an angle over one shoulder. She tugged at the scarf, though it needed no adjusting—nothing she wore ever did. Angela had once thought, as a girl, that Elizabeth probably woke with her hair in perfect order, smelling like Cashmere Bouquet.

"It's nice of you to say," Angela offered. "Rob's helped quite a bit these past few days."

Ruby and Elizabeth both nodded, eyes bouncing through the old bar.

As it turned out, Rob knew some guys looking for extra holiday income. It also turned out that Rob remembered how his superiors had once addressed him in the military, and he'd used similar tactics, pushing the poor guys forward, increasing their speed, making them work harder, more efficiently. Rob's guys had put the ones Angela'd hired to shame.

The women all smiled, thinking of Rob barking out orders. "Like a scene from *An Officer and a Gentleman*," Barbara Lewis commented, before finally carrying her margarita back to her table.

Ruby, Elizabeth, and Angela let out a chorus of laughter.

"You really are down to a few odds and ends," Elizabeth commented. "Drywall's up, paint's drying. All you need to do is take down the painter's tape, add your decorations…"

"I do feel bad that we're going to be interrupting your happy hour," Angela said sadly. The regulars had all decided, one after another, that the get-together in Tom's memory was for the living.

As though to make up for it, Angela offered a plate of toasted marshmallows to the two women, encouraging them to have a bite.

"You're getting better," Ruby managed, fanning her mouth.

Angela warmed at the compliment.

Elizabeth shifted in her chair, frowning. "Now that things are coming together, I think it's safe to say that I won't be here on Christmas Eve."

Angela raised a hand to her cheek, in the same way she would have if she'd just been slapped. "What are you talking about?"

"Pfff," Elizabeth grumbled. "You don't need me here. Not on Christmas Eve. My job is done."

"No, it's not," Ruby argued.

Elizabeth cocked her head and gave her a kind of *get real* look. "My job was to get Angela in here. Last year. To show her what this place could be. Make sure she would want to open it up again, before it was too late and the place got too run-down for anyone to want to save it. Before it fell in after a Midwest wind storm and the bricks got scooped up and thrown away, and we didn't have anyplace to go anymore."

"I thought we agreed," Ruby protested. "It will take all of us working together to reunite people."

"You can't do this to me," Angela begged, leaning over the bar, closer to her aunt. "You absolutely cannot. We all need your help, and I need a ton of moral support. Where am I going to be without you on Christmas Eve? I've always thought of it as our time, ever since I was a little girl. And now—what could potentially be the most special Christmas of all. And you won't be here?"

"Why would you not want to be here to see it all come together?" Ruby challenged. "What's gotten into you?" She sounded hurt, disappointed. Maybe even a little angry.

"Nothing's gotten into me. It's been on my mind for a while now, and I—"

"—am totally transparent," Ruby finished. "Like some crummy old *ghost*." She shoved Elizabeth playfully, until she got a sound close to a giggle out of her.

"Okay, okay!" Elizabeth shouted. "You got me. You win. I'll be here." She offered a slight smile. But Angela wondered why, in that moment, she didn't see the same light in Aunt Elizabeth's eyes—not the familiar twinkle that usually followed the mention of Ruby's Place and Christmas Eve.

The answer came to her as she followed Elizabeth's stare straight to Walter. Walter, who was leaning against the piano.

Walter, who did not chime in as usual when a toast came from the back of the room: "To the ghosts of Christmas past!" Walter, who believed his only son would not be coming. Who was looking at a Christmas in which he would not enjoy a reunion of his own.

Elizabeth and Walter were in the same situation, Angela realized. Elizabeth didn't expect to make a new connection, either. Sometimes, another's unexpected joy made you feel as though you'd already had your something wonderful; it was behind your shoulder, and now, all you could do was think of those who weren't around, those you still missed, those you might never see again. Everyone had one. A hole, a missing spot where someone used to be. No matter how magical Ruby's Place was, it couldn't literally reunite every single person.

Angela suddenly felt ashamed for her lack of understanding—for thinking only of herself.

"Elizabeth—I didn't mean to—I wasn't trying…"

"Pfff," Elizabeth said. "Don't you worry." She patted Angela's hand.

"But I—"

"I'm coming. Case closed," Elizabeth assured them. "Why don't you whip up a hot chocolate for me? I'm suddenly in the mood."

Angela nodded, dragging herself into the kitchen and

feeling more guilty than she ever had before. It was a startling idea that even after life was over, the heart could still break.

32.

RUBY lingered after happy hour had wrapped up completely.

Alone again in her old bar, she stood in view of the mirror behind the top shelf bottles. She smiled at her image—her unlined face and slender body—before raising her arms above her head.

She was a far better dancer now than she had been when audiences stood to applaud and cry out, "Brava!" And not just because she no longer had a body that imposed physical limitations. Being a bartender had taught her a lot about human nature. About the heart. About what motivated people. What they regretted. What they dreamed of. What secrets they told, what secrets they kept. Everything that had happened at the bar—both before and after her death—had given her a new understanding of people. And that changed the way she expressed herself.

She lowered her arms and sighed. Such a shame that all this newfound ability had come to her here, after her life was over.

Ruby doubted there was any way around it, though. Hindsight was 20/20. And perhaps there was no clearer hindsight in the world than that which came after *everything* was over, including breathing.

She leaned her elbows against the bar, thinking of all the beginnings and ever-afters she had lived vicariously through her patrons. What was the biggest lesson that she had learned about human nature? The one lesson that topped them all?

That nothing comes together on its own, magically.

She was not sure any happy ending had ever come into existence without a fair amount of meddling.

She had done quite a bit of meddling herself.

33.

1967

RUBY knew, the moment Elizabeth entered the bar, that her friend wasn't exactly feeling merry and bright. She glared as her eyes adjusted to the candlelight. She grimaced against the carols and she sidestepped an attempted hug from an obviously drunk and happy young man. As Elizabeth slipped out of her coat, a bough of mistletoe appeared over her head. She batted it away and made a beeline for the bar.

She looked like she needed far more than a drink. She'd clearly come for a shot of Ruby's companionship served on the house.

"What's got you down, kid?" Ruby asked, sincerely concerned.

Elizabeth shook her head. "I'm not sure. I'm—" Her

voice trailed.

"Not in the mood? Feeling a little bout of the Scrooge coming on?" Ruby asked. But it wasn't mean-spirited. It was jovial. Ruby had easily fallen into her role as bartender, and had quickly been labeled the best listener in all of Sullivan. Elizabeth had often teased her about knowing more secrets, at that point, than the Ladies' Benevolent Society, who had been gathering and disseminating them for decades. Why, Ruby had to know as many secrets as the night stars, often considered the safest place to put your deepest, darkest wishes.

"Do you ever feel," Elizabeth asked, "like you fought and fought to get somewhere and it wasn't at all what you expected it to be?"

Ruby thought a moment before shaking her head. "Well, no. Wait a minute. I take that back," she said. "Nothing's ever *exactly* like you pictured it would be. Is it?"

Elizabeth sighed, her black velvet suit matching her current dark mood. "I had to fight to prove I was worthy of being in the room. When I started working, I was regarded at first as another skirt. I convinced everyone I wasn't. I've been buying clothes for Graham's Department store for eons, and I do enjoy it, but it's…"

Ruby leaned forward and shouted something at Elizabeth, finishing her sentence for her. But her words were swallowed by a surge of boisterous joy. Good grief, inside Ruby's Place in December, joy came in actual waves. It was a tide that rushed in and swept you up before you had a chance to fasten your life jacket. You could drown in cheers and laughter during the holidays.

Elizabeth frowned; she clearly didn't want anything to do with joy. Not that year.

She shook her head, indicating she hadn't heard Ruby.

"Because it's not yours," Ruby repeated, leaning still closer and speaking louder.

"I'm not sure what you mean," Elizabeth shouted back. "My career isn't mine?"

"I mean you didn't build it from scratch—you don't own it outright. You report to someone else," Ruby explained. "I found that out when I bought this place. I mean, sure, I still have to deal with City Council or the occasional inspector with an ax to grind, but it's different when you're making the big decisions. When your name's on the door. Right?"

Elizabeth shrugged. She still didn't see Ruby's point.

Ruby sighed, put down her martini shaker. "Look at me," she said, arms held wide. "What do you think?"

Elizabeth's eyes bounced over Ruby, taking her in. "Same Ruby, just like always," she said. And to some extent, she was right. Same silver hair, tied into a tight ballerina bun at the top of her head. Same pale pink lipstick. Same full black pants. The main holiday deviations were the gray and black variegated faux fur shirt and red chandelier earrings.

"Same old me since I met you," Ruby corrected. "You picked my outfit for tonight, remember. And you've been dressing me for years."

"I've been dressing lots of people for years," Elizabeth groaned.

"So do it on your own terms. Open your own shop."

"You can't be serious."

"As a heart attack," Ruby claimed. A common phrase in Sullivan, and one she must have heard close to a million times since returning home.

Before Elizabeth could roll her eyes, Ruby said, "I've never had any regrets about what I did. Some people, they see no husband, no kids, they think, oh, she must lead an empty life. That's the farthest thing from the truth. I went after what I wanted—dance, and when that career was over, this place— and I'll never have any regrets about either. What you need is to fill that hole in your heart. Build a place that's all yours. Nobody else's."

Elizabeth's face shifted a bit to reveal that Ruby's words had painted a brilliant picture in her head—perhaps one even accompanied by a sudden, severe surge of desire. But before she could get too carried away, she simply said, "That's a beautiful idea. Really. But I wasn't a famous dancer."

"I wasn't that famous—"

"What I mean is, I'm not somebody with a previous career, somebody who saved, somebody who invested smartly—like you. I don't have the kind of cash that would let me go out and buy—or lease—my own place, open my own business."

Ruby pursed her lips and crossed her arms as a kind of wordless disagreement.

"Don't give me that look."

"You think it was easy for me?" Ruby asked. "Need I remind you?" She pointed to a table behind Elizabeth's shoulder.

Elizabeth turned. There they were, like they were every year—Roy Weber of Weber Electronics, his wife, his (now grown) kids in town for the holiday, his brother-in-law Nick, and Nick's current plus-one—this time, a raven-haired divorcée from Schenectady.

Roy lit a cigarette, scowling at Ruby the entire time.

"That's exactly the kind of thing I'm talking about," Elizabeth said. "It's been—what? Twelve years since you opened? And still that Roy guy has it out for you. Every single time he arranges his own work get-together, he has it over at that tavern off the Interstate. He only comes here because he lost a bet."

"And I get to rub it in his face every single year that I'm making it," Ruby hissed at Elizabeth.

"He doesn't like you," Elizabeth said. "He still doesn't think you should be here. More than a decade later. If you haven't convinced him in twelve years, how am I ever supposed to convince somebody—"

"Why do you have to? Just do it. Open a place. Proof is in the receipts, mostly."

"Because I don't have the funds. I told you. And no one is going to give a loan to a woman."

"I know a guy."

"Sure." Elizabeth picked up her glass of champagne. "Everyone knows a guy."

"I do. Walter at the bank. He's not that way."

"Walter at the bank," Elizabeth repeated.

"Yeah. He's here. Want me to introduce you?"

"Next you're going to tell me he's the poor guy who held the mistletoe over my head when I walked in."

"Nah, that's Dean, who got a promotion and thinks he can take on the world. I'm talking about Walter. *Walter.*" She pointed across the room, at a man seated with a bunch of other business suits.

"I'm at that bank every week," Elizabeth said, "and I get no farther than the redheaded teller. Agnes."

"Will you think about it?"

"I'll think about it," Elizabeth agreed.

"Good," Ruby said, circling around the bar. She stuck her hand in Elizabeth's armpit, knowing firsthand that business propositions were more easily achieved during the holidays. She hauled Elizabeth to her feet and announced, "You can think about it on the way to his table. "

34.

2018

"YES, old girl," Ruby told herself, "you've got to push people." Sometimes, she knew, that meant giving someone a literal shove—like it had with Elizabeth. And sometimes—like it still was with Angela—it meant providing a series of roadblocks.

All along, Ruby and the regulars had continued to play the same games: messing with Angela's plumbing, leaving patches of mold and rotten wood, causing all those electric snafus. Ruby'd learned long ago that if it was all about the bottom line, all about making a buck, people gave up quickly, heading off to find easier means. If it was about something more, though—like it was with Angela—roadblocks only made them fight harder.

So far, it had worked beautifully. At this point, Angela was desperate to get people to the old bar. So desperate, she was willing to host a celebration of life for someone she barely knew. So desperate, she was trying to manipulate a first-love reunion. Playing into town gossip.

Would she have been so industrious had renovations gone a bit smoother? Did she ever stop to think that all her setbacks had also added fuel to the town gossip? Didn't she suspect that Ruby had learned word-of-mouth was by far the best advertisement? And didn't she sense that gossip had already been fanning the flames of the town's curiosity?

In the kitchen, Ruby propped her hands on her hips, staring at what had to be the world's oldest working cooler.

"You ought to be as dead as I am," Ruby reminded the contraption. "I know you pretty well, though, don't I? Every bit as well as I know Angela. I get what makes you—and her—and this town—tick.

"Funny," she added, "how people don't question things that are working. It's the stuff that doesn't do what a person wants that gets futzed with."

She placed her fingers on the handle of the fridge, the same way she might put her hand on a customer's arm to provide a bit of comfort. "Yes, I knew if I kept you working, no one would look too closely at what was keeping you going. And

I knew that meant I'd be able to use that to my advantage."

She crossed to the back of the cooler, taking a look at where the ancient piece of equipment plugged into the wall.

"Time for a little more meddling. One more roadblock. Otherwise, these people around here are going to all miss their happy endings completely."

35.

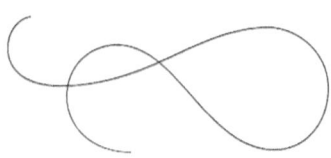

A cardinal swooped down from the sky to land on the sidewalk near Ruby's. He cocked his head, confused by this new activity. Over the past few months, he'd grown accustomed to the noises and patterns of construction. He'd grown used to Angela. But dusk had fallen. And instead of everyone leaving, people were just arriving. The door was open. New noises, new faces appeared, one after another.

Taking up a closer spot on the window ledge, the cardinal could see that Angela had dressed in a long black skirt and a black chenille sweater, a long black and white beaded necklace draped around her neck. She'd swept her hair up, slipped her feet into fancy looking dress shoes.

She was circulating through the room, offering her guests either a Pabst, saying, "Tom's favorite drink," or wine from some high-end California place that had suffered a drought. "A dry spell always makes a sweeter wine," Angela

215

promised.

The cardinal didn't know about that, but he did know that everything tasted sweeter after a long time without: water, sunlight, a stray cookie crumb. Didn't humans know that, too? Did they really need to be told?

The place was packed. Clusters of men with gray hair. Clusters of women wearing kind of hazy, faraway smiles. All of them talking—making far more noise than the birds in early spring. Telling stories. All about someone named Tom.

And then a woman—large glasses, wild blond hair—entered. She was clearly upset. Not crying, but animals didn't cry, either. And faces were never really stoic, regardless of the creature involved. Human, bird, dog—all living things wore their thoughts on their faces. Anyone who didn't think so, anyone who leaned on that term "stoic" wasn't paying attention. Then again, humans rarely did.

Everyone inside the bar flocked to the blond with the glasses, swooping in close. Telling her they were sorry. So sorry.

She was apologizing too. "I'm awfully late." She kept repeating it, though the cardinal wasn't sure why. He'd heard people say it before, say it often. Why humans adhered to such ridiculous social rules, he'd never understand. Made him prize his freedom even more.

From his spot at the window, he watched the fear grow

on the face of the upset girl everyone called "Geena." But they all kept coming right up to her, wrapping their arms around her. Which also seemed strange. He knew approaching an animal that was afraid never got you anything but trouble.

Geena didn't lash out, though. Just another puzzling thing about this night.

"Mrs. Cranston," she called, reaching to hug another woman.

The hug was mutual—it looked like something the women had done many times before. But it also included a fair amount of distrust, like maybe the older woman had bitten the younger one at some point.

That was truly the only kind of distrust the cardinal had ever come to know.

"Beautiful brooch," Geena said, pointing to a shiny green chunk of glass on Mrs. Cranston's shoulder.

"Reminds me of your dad," the woman said, which alarmed Geena.

"Wh—why?" she asked. "Did Dad give it to you?"

But Mrs. Cranston ignored her question. She leaned closer, offering a knowing smile. "You know, Angela never would have gotten all this together in time without Rob's help."

Geena looked confused. Even more upset. "Rob?"

And suddenly, there was a burst of noise. Together, the

people inside were behaving like a pack. Pushing Geena toward the front of the room. "A toast!" a few shouted. Humans had an incessant need to give special reason to their gatherings.

Their scents bled through the glass. The room smelled hot—like too many bodies. Normally, this would have been a signal for him to take flight. But he stayed, too interested to leave. And besides, no one was paying any attention to him.

Behind him, a truck pulled to a stop. "Hey, Rob," a man called out as he slammed the driver door shut.

Another man still crossing the street—this one in a bluebird-colored cap—held up a large cardboard box rather than wave. "No celebration for Tom would be complete without these," he shouted back.

"What are they?"

"L'Amour paperbacks. Every single one I had in my shop. I had no idea how many I'd stockpiled thinking Tom'd come in wanting a new read. Two and three copies of some, because Tom sometimes read his favorites until they fell apart. I thought everyone who comes tonight should take one home. Read and remember our friend."

"That's great!" the man from the truck said loudly, patting this Rob person on his back.

As the two of them walked in, the man shouted, "Hey! Looka who's here," and turned himself into a human arrow as he jabbed his index finger down toward the top of Rob's head.

Everyone in the room turned.

And then it was back and forth—looking at Geena, then looking at Rob. Looking at Geena, looking at Rob. Geena, holding her wineglass shoulder-height in the midst of an awkward toast. Rob, weighed down by his bulging box of paperbacks.

The tension between the two was undeniable. Even the snooping cardinal felt it. Surely the humans felt it, too. The pressure of it all hummed and throbbed.

Rob nodded once at Geena. She took a deep breath and nodded back. A tiny recognition.

The cardinal flapped his wings, sending his feathers ruffling. He felt the turmoil in the atmosphere the same way he could feel a storm rolling in.

He could sense that everyone had come to say goodbye. It seemed so strange. All these people the cardinal had never seen together at once, they'd flocked to Ruby's to say goodbye? Goodbye and not hello?

And yet, it was true. He knew it was.

But Rob and Geena, weren't they trying to say the opposite of goodbye? Wasn't there a pull toward each other? Wasn't that adding to the horrible, horrible pressure?

"Dad wasn't one—wasn't..." Geena struggled, pushing

219

her hair away from her face. "Wasn't—one who would ever want to be the guest of honor, win awards. He hated birthday parties."

A few people laughed in knowing agreement.

"I do think, though, that he would have loved this get-together, so raise your glass and—"

Geena was cut short by an explosion. A crunch and crash from the kitchen.

Squeals and shouts burst as the bar began to fill with a gush of unwelcome water.

36.

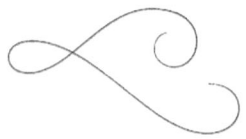

"MY mom was there last night when it happened," Zoe Vega remarked as she dragged a bottle of heartburn medication across the scanner at the Walgreens at the edge of town.

It was awfully busy now that Christmas was edging closer—less than a couple of blinks away. People were flocking to buy last-minute candy and stocking stuffers and gift cards for their bosses and neighbors and postal workers and the teaching assistants at their kids' schools. And since she was the last girl in the pecking order—barely seventeen, a part-time new hire—she was given the crummiest hours. Mostly the seven to eleven shift at night, much to her dad's chagrin. Every night she worked, she came home to find him still in the living room, pretending to watch TV. When she asked, he never seemed to know the storylines of the movies that were

221

on—sometimes, he didn't even know the title. Which lead her to believe he'd really been watching that oh-so-dramatic show The Ticking Clock.

Finally, though—some relatively decent hours. An afternoon for once. She needed to bolt as soon as her shift was up so that she could finish her history paper.

For now, though, Zoe relished her ability to tell her story...over and over again.

"I hear it was quite the scene!" Zoe's customer—Mrs. Hawkins, the wife of a long-time City Council member—hissed, tugging a few last-minute stuffed animals and knock-off Barbies from her shopping cart.

"Yeah, you know," Zoe went on, scanning a plush snowman doll, "it was out of nowhere. Like they were having this thing for Tom, and *kaploosh*!" She illustrated by pantomiming rushing flood waters. "Place was underwater in a matter of seconds."

"The *whole* place?" Mrs. Hawkins pressed as Zoe dropped the snowman into a plastic sack.

"Well. The whole floor. Came from this giant refrigerator thing in the back. I don't know why it had water."

"Probably made ice," Mrs. Hawkins suggested.

"Yeah, probably. I don't think there was really much else they could do except turn the water valve off and set up these pump things."

"Like a sump pump?"

Zoe shrugged. Details such as these rarely penetrated the seventeen-year-old mind. "All I know is, some people promised they'd be back out there today. To help the lady who bought the place."

"At least everybody got a chance to get together, tell their stories, grieve."

"But the *really* weird thing is *this*."

Zoe stopped ringing items. She leaned over the checkout counter to murmur, "Everyone started saying as soon as they got to Ruby's that Tom had to be rolling in his grave. Because he didn't want a funeral and maybe not even a celebration of his life. And how, if it was in his power, he'd stop that crummy party in its *tracks*."

"They did."

"Yes. And then when the flood happened, everybody said, 'It's Tom. Getting rid of us.'"

"Ooh, come on, now," Mrs. Hawkins said, making a face.

Zoe's dark hair began to fall from her French braid. "I know. It sounds like baloney. But here's the thing: My dad's one of the construction guys who's been working on that place *forever*. And he says that the fridge has been kind of limping along, even though it shouldn't be working at all. Like there's some kind of extra weird force powering it, right? For *months*."

"Tom didn't die that long ago, though," Mrs. Hawkins said, her mouth stretched into one of those *you're pulling my leg* grins. "Not months. Just a few days."

"Yeah, well…" Zoe's eyes shifted back and forth as she tried to account for this sudden discrepancy in her story. "Dad says there was always something strange about that place. You know? And then the water bursts! Like on cue? All I'm saying is, it sure is weird."

"Seems so," Mrs. Hawkins agreed, grabbing a few loaded plastic sacks into her fist and dropping them into her cart.

"Sure do hope they get the place cleaned up in time for the Christmas Eve opening," Zoe remarked.

"Why the interest? Ruby's is some old bar—one that was open way before your time."

"You kidding? With all that weird stuff going on, I gotta see this place for myself."

37.

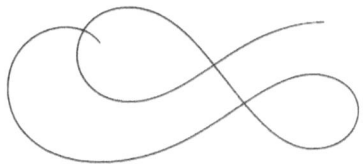

A man didn't serve in the military without learning a thing or two about wounds. What healed on its own and what needed stitches. How you managed a pain that would most likely be part of you from then on, pulsing through every single day of civilian life.

The service also taught a person about the other kind of wounds—the kind that happened inside, that never bled, that left scars no one could ever see. Fear and regret were wounds. So were near-misses. Even looking forward to a much-needed leave only to have it snatched away. Feeling close enough to taste home and then being forced to admit, only moments later, that it was still every bit as out of reach as ever.

It sounded like a small thing. But Rob knew firsthand that when you watched something you almost had slip away, it often turned into something you couldn't get out of your mind—it became a far greater agony than if you'd never had the chance at all.

Rob had seen Geena twice by that point—once on the sidewalk, once at Ruby's. Both times, he'd wanted to talk to her, only to have his chance ripped away. Only to find himself at home, in bed, staring into the ceiling, never having said a single word to her.

That busted pipe—the one that had sent everyone scattering, with Rob unable to locate Geena anywhere, not for the rest of the night—was his breaking point. He had no more room inside for a what-if. For a might-have-been. He didn't want to have to carry a reopened wound, even one he could try to convince himself was too old to become reinfected. Why should he, when he could so easily find a remedy?

So when Rob piled into his truck that morning, he didn't drive straight out to Ruby's, even though he'd promised he'd be there, first thing, to finish cleaning the place up. Nor did he drive out to Maria's to pick up Justin, who'd promised to work the counter at The Page Turner while Rob was across the street helping Angela. Instead, Rob took a path he hadn't been down for three decades.

Sullivan had received a light dusting of snow the night before. It made the town look as quaint as a Christmas card.

The old gas station on the corner of Maple was gone. The same station where Rob had once stolen the occasional pack of underage cigarettes. Nothing was left of it anymore but a cracked parking lot. At least, Rob imagined it was cracked. He didn't know for sure, because of the snow. Funny, he caught himself thinking, how snow acted a little like a scab, concealing the town's tiny little fissures and crumbling places.

Even towns, he realized, suffered wounds.

Ahead, he could make out the sharply pitched roof of the Burger Shack—the same place where he and Geena had celebrated with their first shared birthday dinner, their birthdays being a week apart in October. "What's it feel like dating an older man?" he'd teased her during that week when his age had been one digit higher than hers. Every single year thereafter, he'd teased her about it, too. It had been their game—he'd even given her a few gag gifts, little girl barrettes and elementary-school folders with unicorns, that sort of thing. At least, until she'd given him one of those old-man canes with the large flexible rubber foot for stability.

The Shack had been replaced by some fancy coffee shop. It seemed about as out of place along this stretch of Sullivan as a woman in a ball gown shopping the aisles of the Dollar General.

So much had changed since he'd driven this way. Not that he'd been purposefully avoiding the area. Just hadn't had reason to come out. After all, his home and business were the other direction.

You sure about that? he asked himself. *You sure you weren't trying to avoid suffering the pain of your most torturous near-miss? A thing that almost was, could have been—and wasn't?*

He squirmed against the bench seat. Last month, he would have considered the idea preposterous. Now, he wasn't so sure.

Geena's mother didn't live in town anymore. But it was still the house Geena's family had all shared—the house where she'd lived when she was born and the house where she spent most of her weekends and holiday breaks and summers, the house where Tom had always lived—that Rob remembered most clearly.

He turned down the familiar street and found himself slowing near a tree where he and Geena had once made out during a summer rainstorm. It had been an accident, really—the two of them out for a picnic, getting caught in the rain. Their lips had brushed as they'd started to get up from their spot between the tree's gnarled roots—and Rob might have let it go at that, but Geena had tugged him closer. He needed to tell her they'd fry if lightning struck. He knew that even then. But he hadn't said anything. He wasn't sure how long it had lasted—maybe a couple of minutes, maybe three hours—thunder rippling against the sky, getting wetter and wetter, their lips tangling. It was wild and it shouldn't have happened. But there they were, just the same. Two kids the right age to chase danger, dance with the lightning.

That afternoon in the storm summed up who they'd been back then. *Rob & Geena 4Ever.*

The old oak was nearly dead now. Most of its branches gone, the remaining ones dying. Probably hit by the ice storm they'd had a few years back. After a certain point, the entire trunk would rot and it would come down easier. Crumble. Another victim of an ever-changing landscape.

He rounded another corner and pulled to the curb. Opened his door and tugged his Royals cap down lower on his forehead. Maybe it was to keep the snowflakes from getting in his eyelashes, maybe to hide the burst of emotion he felt. His entire youth suddenly seemed closer than it had in ages.

The snow crunched as he trudged up the front walk lined with decorative poinsettias. He brushed a few flakes from his shoulders even as the snow continued to fall—a useless attempt, he knew, but that didn't stop him.

Before stepping onto the porch, he paused, taking a moment to collect himself. He thought he heard a distant hum of a generator. Maybe some unlucky soul had suffered an outage—it wouldn't be out of the question, all those aging trees in the area, all the old sagging power lines. Everyone in town had just-in-case generators. Rob himself had one. Wouldn't have ever caught himself without, not after the storm everyone still referred to as the Big One of '87. Three and a half feet in less than twenty-four hours. Wound up knocking out nearly every house for the better part of two weeks.

Rob and Geena had been skating on Miller's Pond when it really started to come down. By the time he'd walked her to the door, the streets were already completely covered—some too deep to maneuver. They'd had to dig his Caprice out twice to get her home. They'd arrived wet and cold, muscles on fire.

But Rob had done it—he'd gotten Geena home with a little room to spare before her curfew. He'd succeeded in giving Tom nothing to complain about, for once.

He'd held her hand to make sure she didn't slip on the porch steps.

The front door had flown open, exposing Tom's perturbed expression.

Geena scampered inside.

Rob raised a hand in a goodnight wave.

Before Rob could leave, though, Tom had uncharacteristically reached out, grabbed him by the arm, and dragged him inside the house.

38.

1987

"DID you get called in?" Geena asked, staring at her dad's uniform. "I thought you had the night off."

"I was coming to look for you," Tom barked.

"I'm a little early, though, aren't I? Getting her home, I mean?" Rob checked his watch, even though he already knew the time. "Fifteen minutes before her curfew." He twisted his wrist to show him. "My watch isn't slow, is it?" he asked, pretending not to understand. But he knew what Tom was up to. He knew exactly why he'd chosen the uniform. When Tom found Geena and Rob, wherever they were, Tom could grab Rob up by the scruff of his neck, and it would look like Rob was being hauled in for wrongdoing. It would not look like an overprotective father annoyed with the idea of his little girl

231

getting all mixed up with a boy with a bit of a troublemaker reputation. At least, not while he was wearing his blues. Not with his badge visible.

"Sir?" Rob pressed.

"What's the deal, Dad?" Geena snarled, throwing her weight onto one hip, glaring at her father.

"I was worried. Snow's piling up. Wrecks all over town."

"Which is why we started back early," Rob explained. "I knew it'd take longer to drive here, as hard as it was coming down. Wanted to make sure I had her back before curfew—and in one piece. Can't afford catastrophes this close to Christmas, right?"

Tom shot a glare of his own at Rob, hot enough to melt any remaining snowflakes in Rob's hair.

"Anyway, I should head out," Rob said, attempting his escape. "I've got a slick drive ahead of me. Getting back home will be tricky…" He turned for the door, but Geena stopped him.

"If it's getting bad, shouldn't he stay?" Geena pressed.

"Yes. Well. I—" Tom stuttered.

"Dad!" Geena shouted. "He should *stay awhile*. Right? Until they can plow the streets?"

"It's okay. I think I can make it," Rob tried.

"No," Tom suddenly said, his voice the kind of stern

no teenager would ever dare argue with. "I think she's right."

They all shed their coats in the front hall. Tom hung them on the coat rack in the corner. Rob felt strangely hemmed-in by that action—like somehow, Tom had shoved *him* into a tiny little confined space in the corner to torture him.

"I'd better call my folks, let them know where I am," Rob said, making his way across the living room, toward the kitchen.

He was less than halfway across the rug when the lights died.

"Guess we're in for a dark night," Rob muttered, growing a little more nervous with every single tick of some unseen living room clock.

"Not with Dad's emergency lantern supply," Geena announced, as though they were all playing some fun little game of make-believe.

Rob didn't think this was fun. And the snow outside was definitely not made up. Or tapering off. At all.

"Tell your folks you'll spend the night," Tom called as Rob picked up the receiver from the wall phone. "You'll sleep on the couch."

Rob complied, barely listening to the response on the other end.

"What'd they say?" Geena asked, placing battery-powered lanterns on the table. She turned them on, casting a kind of creepy, shadowy, muted light throughout the kitchen.

"Said they can think of far worse places to be during a blizzard than a police officer's house."

Geena smiled, happy to be on this grand adventure.

"Got a—radio—or something?" Rob asked. He scratched the back of his neck, anxious to get a little slice of relief, some break from the obvious tension. Did Geena really not feel it?

"How about Monopoly?" Geena announced. "I bet we still have the board upstairs…"

She raced off, leaving Rob and Tom alone in the kitchen with the gourd wallpaper Geena's mother had picked out, the same Tom had never bothered to replace.

"She has no idea where that board is," Tom said. "Why don't you take a seat? Better make yourself comfortable. I think we're in for quite the long haul."

Rob nodded, sliding into a seat on the far side of the table, closest to the sliding glass door.

Tom took the seat across from him.

Still, the living room clock ticked.

The snow on the other side of the kitchen door continued to fall.

The wind made slapping sounds against the back of the

house.

Rob picked at a cuticle.

Tom shot Rob a series of dirty looks, one right after another.

"Geena's sixteen," Tom finally began.

Rob wondered if he was going to leave his uniform on all night.

"Yessir," Rob finally croaked, when it became clear Tom was waiting for some sort of response.

"She's in contention to be valedictorian."

"I figured."

"You did."

Rob nodded. "It would only make sense, sir. She's the smartest girl in the class."

Tom sighed. "She has a lot going for her."

"Yes."

"I'm not convinced you're good for her."

"I might not be."

Tom scowled at Rob in a way that said he wasn't quite sure what to make of this bit of honesty. "I can't disallow it. Her seeing you, I mean. I know that. She's got a mind of her own. But I don't care for it, either."

Rob nodded. "I know you don't. But I'm going to convince you otherwise."

Tom leaned back into his chair. His face twisted into one of those expressions adults wore when they came into contact with complete and total naïveté. "You have no idea what kind of deck is stacked against you."

"I think I do. It doesn't matter how long it'll take. I'll convince you."

Tom offered a crocodile smile. "People your age say that kind of thing, and I honestly think you do believe you mean it. But I also think that in your mind, a month is a really long time."

Rob shrugged. "How long do you think it'll take?"

"If you convinced me you were good for her in less than thirty years, it would be a miracle. That's the kind of convincing I need here."

Rob straightened up and offered his hand for Tom to shake. "Deal," he said. The lanterns cast a dim light down his arm. He figured it was also highlighting the dirty blond tips of his long hair and the hope filling his eyes.

Tom reached across the table to shake his hand.

"I found it!" Geena shouted, bounding back down the stairs.

The two men pulled away from each other. The subject had officially been dropped for the duration of the storm.

236

39.

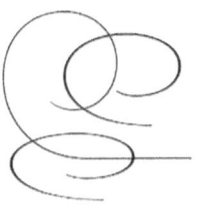

2018

GEENA was still lacing up her waterproof boots when the doorbell rang. Was it Mrs. Cranston? She hoped so. She hadn't had a chance to talk to her last night—and there were so many questions about her and her father that she wanted to ask. Then again, Geena hadn't had a chance to talk to much of anyone last night. Everyone had kind of scattered, like marbles rolling across the floor.

She threw the door open, shocked to find a familiar face on the porch.

"Hey," she said.

"Hey."

They stared at each other. Geena was frozen, unsure

what to say next.

"Snow's picking up," Rob finally managed. "Hope it doesn't turn into a Big One."

"Like in '87," Geena said.

"Yeah."

They fell quiet again.

"I thought—maybe you'd like a ride over to Ruby's?" Rob offered. "I figured you'd be going. From the way you're dressed," he went on, pointing at her jeans and her boots, "I was right. I thought—why not ride together? Especially—with the snow—and everything. Might get slick later."

"That's a good idea," Geena mumbled, taking a step back in a way that invited him in.

She wasn't sure what to do after that. She felt a little disoriented—not unpleasantly so—but was having trouble figuring out her next move.

"Coffee?" Rob asked.

He smiled, and Geena found that breathing got instantly harder. That crooked smile had made her weak in the knees way back then and it was doing a pretty good job of befuddling her now.

Weak in the knees, she scolded herself. *Nice cliché, there, professor.*

Still, she couldn't stop staring. It was the same Rob, all

right—even though his hair was grayer and he had little smile lines around his mouth.

Wrinkles had always looked to Geena like the corners of pages that had been dog-eared. Special passages in a favorite book that the owner wanted to be able to find again easily.

She wondered if she was one of Rob's.

"The coffee?" he asked, when the staring at him went on a little too long.

"Right."

She raced through the living room, Rob following several steps behind.

"Place looks the same," he observed.

"Yeah, Dad was a creature of habit," Geena admitted.

"Surprised he never sold it, moved someplace smaller," Rob said. "Even has the same sofa in the living room. Man, I remember having to sit on that thing, waiting for you to come downstairs—attempting some kind of halfway decent conversation with Tom."

Geena turned her attention toward opening the can of coffee without spilling grounds everywhere.

But the lid fought her—the silly plastic lid. The lip of the can was dented, and the lid had been forced on, and now, for some reason, it refused to peel back. At that moment, with Rob there unannounced and her father the protector gone, with

Christmas coming and her father's stocking dangling from the mantel and the gifts he'd never unwrap still stacked under the tree and the years stretched before her and this aching, festering hole inside—it felt like the entire world was closing in on her, squeezing tighter and tighter.

She let out a frustrated yelp and slammed the can on the counter.

Before she could begin to collect herself or apologize, offer a weak *I've been so frazzled lately*, two arms were wrapping around her, hugging her.

She turned, wrapping her arms around Rob, hugging him back.

Holding onto Rob, she felt eighteen, in the front seat of that crummy old Caprice. Heat blowing on her from the dash, Skid Row playing on the radio.

Suddenly, through her tears, she was unleashing it all. Everything that she'd dreamed of being able to say out loud: about the shock of losing her father, about how the world looked different, almost menacing sometimes, about how much easier it had been to be tough when she knew she had her dad for backup. She stopped short of telling him about Mrs. Cranston. That felt like her father's business. It felt like it wasn't hers to share.

Rob listened. As she'd always known he would. "You

240

know," he said, "in the end, he was one of my favorite people. Isn't that funny? The guy who used to give me the world's hardest time. The guy who hated my guts until a couple of years ago. The guy I used to dread seeing. Later on, he was the one I looked forward to seeing maybe even more than anyone."

When she finally pulled away, Rob's eyes were wet, too.

"I guess Dad left an empty place in just about everybody, didn't he?" Geena asked.

"He did at that," Rob said, wiping his face. "Kinda feels like he's still putting me through the ringer." He reached up to tuck her hair behind her ear; Geena warmed at the familiar gesture.

He pointed at the front of her sweater. "Hey. That's my necklace," he said.

Geena wrapped her fist around the nail. She hadn't taken the silly thing off since unearthing it from the Reebok box.

Maybe it was because she'd already opened up to Rob, telling him about her father. But she suddenly had no problem blurting, "Why'd you stop writing?"

"I didn't. You did."

"No—mine was the last letter."

"I don't remember it that way. Maybe I didn't get it. And besides, why would it have to be one-for-one? If you really wanted to hear from me, and I hadn't written, why didn't you just write again?"

Geena frowned. "Because—you—I'm not sure."

"Why didn't you come?" he asked, before she could untangle her thoughts from their long-lost letter writing.

"When? To what?"

"My homecoming party. When I came back from the service."

"Your—you mean the one twenty-some-odd years ago?"

"Yeah."

"I did," Geena said. "You had a date. So I left without saying anything to you. Are you going to tell me she was no big deal? That you would have ditched her to spend your homecoming with me?"

Rob shrugged. "I kinda married her."

"Well, now I'm *really* glad I didn't go in."

"I divorced her later, though."

Geena snorted. "Do you want a gold star? My congratulations?"

Rob laughed. "I missed you, you know. Didn't even really know how much until about a minute ago. This." He pointed back and forth from himself to Geena, referencing the kind-hearted teasing, the playful exchange they'd fallen into effortlessly.

242

"Yeah," Geena said. "Same here."

Could it be true? Could some things really never fade?

She reached again for the coffee, finding that she was now able to peel the lid back easily. "Take your dumb coat off, already."

"You don't have to make that, you know."

"I will. We'll take it with us. Maybe stop for a couple dozen donuts along the way."

"You think Angela can't make coffee?"

"That's not the point. She tried to help me. I'd like to return the favor." Her eyes grew hazy.

"What're you thinking?"

Geena tugged on her lip, anticipating he'd tease her if she came clean. But she said it anyway. "Maybe it was lucky for us that the pipe broke."

He thought about it a moment. "I guess—generally speaking—when most people see each other again after thirty years, they don't start blubbering all over each other's shoulders in public. Falling apart is generally left for the privacy of a father's kitchen."

"I didn't *fall apart*," Geena corrected.

"Mmm-hmm. A little bit, you did."

Geena rolled her eyes, still loving their instant rapport. The fun banter that had fueled the Rob and Geena of Sullivan sidewalk fame was still alive. It didn't completely erase the sadness of losing her father, but it definitely helped. Made it a bit more manageable. Something she wasn't having to carry around all on her own. Not if she had someone like this— someone who didn't require her to be polite or professional or polished. Someone who'd accepted her years ago, and didn't mind or judge when she cracked a bit beneath whatever weight life had decided to unload on her. After all this time, it was like he'd known she needed this very thing: a chance to lean. A kind, warm, welcoming hand. His friendship.

Her heart gushed, spewing far more than that busted pipe at Ruby's Place. It all poured out: lost time and youth and promises and memories and unanswered questions...and love. Every old affection she'd ever felt for Rob—those feelings had gone nowhere. Could new affections form? She didn't know for sure, but Rob had come. He was here. And somehow, in the midst of her father's ending—an end that required she admit her youth was officially long gone—here it was, a beginning and a memory and a slice of that long-gone youth, somehow all wrapped up into the same shiny present.

"Seriously, though. Does this all feel a little weirdly providential?" she asked.

"What, like there's some other hand in this?" Rob asked.

244

Geena shrugged, feeling silly. Rob didn't know her father had sent her to The Page Turner. Now, she was almost embarrassed to tell him.

"So you think there's something left, do you?" Rob asked. His eyes twinkled to reveal he knew the answer, but was waiting to hear what kind of wisecrack she'd unleash next.

"Don't act like I'm the one who's pining. You're the one who remembers how to get to my father's house in a snowstorm."

"You're the one still wearing my necklace," Rob said, leaning closer to her. "Even though you're still kind of out of my league."

"I was never out of your league."

"Yes, you were."

"You never answered my question," Geena said, using her best professor voice. "*Was* that pipe breaking kind of providential?" Their faces had grown close enough at that point to feel his breath on her face.

"Yeah. Maybe it was all orchestrated by an angel. Or the devil himself," Rob joked. Quickly—as though to keep from second-guessing himself—he kissed her and pulled her close again.

40.

ALL it took was Rob and Geena showing up together at Ruby's Place that morning—and suddenly, gossip had legs. It traveled down a snow-dusted Main Street. It knocked on frozen windows. It buzzed through cell phones. Kelly overheard conversations as she shelved books. Zoe repeated snatches as she scanned items at Walgreens. All the Mrs. Hawkinses and the Scott Drummonds, the Pamelas and the Susans in their morning driveways, the cashiers at The Red Apple grocery, the attendant at the gas station—every one of them—had some little tidbit to share, to pass along, to exchange for something new:

Shhhhhh. Let me tell you! You're not going to believe it...

It's about Ruby's Place. *You* know the one. Don't you? It's that old bar being renovated.

Have you heard what's going on inside?

No, I'm not talking about the get-together for Tom Barister.

Haven't you heard about Rob and Geena? *Geena*, I said, Tom's daughter. Well, they were high school sweethearts, don't you know.

Oh, yeah, yeah. He was the troublemaker with that awful old car. She was the smart one.

Everyone's been rooting for them to get back together. You too? Of course you have been.

Well, get this: they were *there*. Rob and Geena. At the same time. To help with the cleanup. Zoe's mom was there and *she* said that every single time they looked at each other, it was fireworks. The giant kind that cover an entire city sky.

That right? Like old times, eh?

Sally said…oh, you know Sally. The one who works the concession stand at the movie theater. Yes, *that* Sally. She said later on they had dinner at the diner and Rob actually reached across the table and touched Geena's hand.

I'm not making this up.

Oh, yes, and Kimberly—Kimberly Tan—she saw them together at The Page Turner. Rob was closing up for the night *early*, if you know what I mean.

What for? They used to go on dates there, to the bookstore.

Yeah, I know. Kimberly said looking at the two of them makes you feel like time's rewound, somehow. Like your own younger you isn't so far away.

Isn't that Rob something? Isn't it thoughtful of him to be there for Geena?

I saw Geena with Justin. Rob's son. Out on the street. So nice to see her meet his son.

My friend Charlie—oh, you've met Charlie, he drives that Coke delivery truck. Right. He heard Rob even asked Geena to the grand opening.

No, that's not right. Someone told me she asked him.

Well. Regardless. They're going to be there. That's a sure thing.

Don't you think they were made for each other?

So sweet.

After all that time.

Sometimes, things are just *right*. No matter how long it's been.

I hear, when they're together, they make everyone around them smile. Kind of get whisked away watching it. The same way an old song or a smell can whisk you away, right? Rob and Geena—they're like a time capsule. You see them, and you remember what it was like for *you*.

That's what everyone is saying.

248

HOLLY SCHINDLER

You're going to be at Ruby's on Christmas Eve, aren't you? You better get there early—bet the whole town shows up to get a glimpse of them. Rob and Geena.

You bet I'll be there. I wouldn't miss it for the world.

41.

S NOW began to fall in earnest on Christmas Eve morning. It no longer simply trickled or lazily swirled through the air. *Dumped*—that was more like it. It forced Angela to turn on her windshield wipers as she steered her car onto the main thoroughfare. It blanketed tree branches and power lines as she snaked her way closer to the old business district. By the time she arrived at Ruby's Place, she found the snow had completely concealed the yellow lines of the parking spaces.

Angela parked by lining her car up with one of the streetlights nearest the bar's entrance. She popped her door and dragged her foot across the ground. "Got to be at least another two inches already," she muttered.

Her stomach knotted. Her stomach had been doing an incredible job of tying knots lately. This was one of those sailor knots, something that was intended to be tied and never come undone again.

250

She dragged herself inside, where the fully decorated interior of the bar—somewhat miraculously—was ready for its grand reopening. Tables had been draped in linen cloths. Red candles stood ready to be lit. Tinsel circled the mirror behind the bar. Pourer caps topped every open bottle of liquor. The piano had been tuned.

Outside, the old neon "Ruby's Place" sign had been rehung. All it needed was a flick of the switch.

Still, though, the snow continued to fall—at times, the spaces between flakes would widen. It would slow to what could be described as mere flurries. But just when Angela had started to believe it was actually maybe possibly coming to an end, it would pick up all over again.

Three inches. Four.

Angela paced and the hours dragged.

Early in the afternoon, the Sullivan snowplow drove past, spraying the sidewalk out front—the same area outside the entrance she had attempted to keep clean, brushing the flakes away once an hour with her broom. But Angela was so grateful, she lunged out of her bright green door and waved at the driver. "Are you clearing all the main roads?" she called. "Are you doing any of the side streets?"

He only honked back. Two quick beeps.

"Come back!" she called. "For our opening—"

But he was too far down the street to hear her.

Ruby was shaking her head at Angela as she pulled herself back inside. "Worrying gets you nowhere," she warned, as though time spent pacing was wasted on Angela's part. But Angela could detect fear in Ruby's eyes, too.

They were both wondering the same thing: What if the snow kept people away? What if the remodeling crew and the former police officers who had worked beside Tom—the same group who had helped out after the burst-pipe fiasco—didn't come, even after they'd promised to be here? What if they didn't realize that showing up was the best thing they could do for her, far better than mopping up her minor flood? Their presence was the not-so-secret ingredient that would make this night a success.

People. Angela needed people. Lots of them. Not snow.

Her two frozen cooks arrived, which made Angela clap with delight. "Must not be too bad out there," she said. "Roads are clear, eh?"

But the roommates only shrugged, explaining they lived close enough to walk. So they'd left their cars in the garage and stayed away from any main road, choosing a shortcut through a maze of covered overpasses and a heated shopping center. "Why chance it?" was how one of them put it.

What a terrible sentence. What a rotten thing to say.

What if everyone else looked out their windows and said, "Why chance it?" What if they kicked off their shoes and had a homebound Christmas Eve?

At four, the regulars began to filter in, dressed in their holiday finest.

"You guys are early," Angela remarked.

"This is a special night," Walter announced. "New customers. Old friends. Reunions. Reconciliations! Who wouldn't want to get here early for that?"

Sure. Customers. Reunions. Angela's doubts were piling up like the snow covering her car outside. Frankly, the regulars didn't seem all that certain, either. They sat quietly, eyes trained toward the front window.

At four-thirty, a knock came to the door, causing the entire bar to jump collectively.

Angela raced to answer. Rob stood in the doorway. "One door greeter extraordinaire," he announced, bowing at the waist. He'd gotten a haircut, Angela noted. And he was wearing a black wool topcoat—the kind of thing Cary Grant himself might have worn as he flashed his signature smile across the big screen.

Geena's face appeared behind Rob's shoulder.

"Hope you don't mind me showing up early, too," she said. "I was coming with Rob, and—I thought maybe you might need another hand. I'm no bartender, but I could maybe help deliver drinks, if you need me to."

"Pleased as punch," Angela announced. And added with a wink, "Pun intended."

She'd known they planned to show up together. But was it enough? Doubt was suffocating her.

Rob hung up his topcoat, revealing a tuxedo jacket and faded jeans. As for Geena, beneath her black trench, she wore a midnight blue dress with long sleeves, which she'd complemented with velvet heels and a large red necklace.

"Relics from the '90s," Geena admitted when she caught Angela eyeing her outfit. "Treasures from the back of my old closet. I hoped they were just vintage enough to be fashionable again."

"Not bad," Elizabeth said, walking around Geena. "Skirt could be maybe an inch longer."

But Geena, unaware she had been critiqued by an expert, simply tossed her wild hair from her face, pushed her large round glasses higher onto her nose, and asked, "Where do we start?"

Angela and Elizabeth exchanged troubled glances. Geena hadn't heard Elizabeth speaking to her. And she didn't see her now.

Judging by the way Rob simply took Geena's coat,

nearly knocking Evie over as he carried it through the Employees Only door, he didn't see any of the regulars, either.

Angela had been warned to expect as much. In fact, she had been told more than once that a big chunk of the night's revelers would never see any of them.

It only seemed logical at the time. She had herself seen the regulars the same way she saw her bedroom when she opened her eyes first thing in the morning. No real conscious effort had been required on her end. There had been no real trick to it. So surely, either you'd see or you wouldn't.

But Rob and Geena? *They* couldn't see them? That couldn't be a good sign. If no one saw the regulars—if no one had a reunion—then Ruby's wasn't the magical place Angela always believed it was. It was another humdrum place to grab a beer. No different than any other bar.

Which also meant that no one would ever have a special reason to visit. No strange, mystical stories would circulate. Ruby's would not be a legend.

She didn't want to be frightened. Or a worrywart. Or a pessimist. But she could not quit wringing her hands. She could not stop dark thoughts from swirling through her mind.

Angela gave Geena a tray and a crash course on how the bar was set up, where to pick up mixed cocktails. She pointed to the tables, giving Rob tips on how to seat customers. But her hands shook the entire time.

Rob nodded to a clock on the far wall. "Almost five o'clock," he announced, his eyes shimmering. "Happy hour. Right?"

Angela forced a smile. But it was entirely possible that they were about to be disappointed. People were creatures of habit, and everyone in Sullivan had been out of the habit of spending Christmas Eve at Ruby's for decades.

And besides, it was still snowing. But living rooms were warm. Decorated trees were sparkling. Presents were waiting.

Why would we need to be anyplace but here? Why chance it? So cold and slick and awful outside.

Angela crossed her fingers and slowly edged toward the door. She glanced once over her shoulder, at Ruby and Elizabeth.

"Go for it, kid," Ruby said, giving her a thumbs-up.

Angela drank in the warmth of the nickname—previously reserved for the ultra-successful Elizabeth—knowing it could also be the last time she heard Ruby use it on her. Knowing that they could be mere moments from an entire year's worth of work going completely belly-up.

Angela turned on the neon "Ruby's Place" sign. Through the front window, she could see the red glow wash against the sidewalk below. They were officially open for business.

256

She unlocked the door.

42.

A shivering man stood maybe a foot from Ruby's entrance, attempting to take shelter under the front awning.

"Scott!" Angela exclaimed with surprise. She was so flabbergasted, she didn't think about letting him in. Instead, she stepped outside the front door to join him.

He smiled. "Well, I approved your loan, so I had to make sure the place got open on time and on the right foot. Even convinced my family to cancel the Colorado trip to be here."

"You did?"

"Sure. They're keeping warm in the car." He turned and waved to a blue EcoSport parked across the street. "From all the talk going around, I figured we'd need to get here early. I'm not the only one who thought so. Obviously." He took a step back to give her an unobstructed view.

258

Angela craned her neck to find that a line stretched down the street and around the corner—out of sight. The city plow had piled mounds of snow on the sidewalk, leaving everyone to stand on the street itself. But they weren't blocking traffic; instead, cars were snaking down the empty lane, all of them heading in the same direction: *toward* Ruby's Place. Though parking spots were at a premium, horns weren't blared in annoyance. They simply tooted in greeting. Arms were raised as the people of Sullivan waved. "Merry Christmas!" they shouted. "See you inside!"

"You don't think anybody's going to be upset that we're parking in all the other businesses' lots, do you?" Scott asked. "Especially since everybody else is closed? I know the bank won't mind, but that's already full."

Angela stuttered. "W—I—"

"I love that you brought the old sign back," Scott said, head tipped back, eyes aimed skyward. "No other sign says Ruby's like that one. Shines bright as the North Star."

"Invite them *in* dear," came Elizabeth's shout from inside.

Angela flinched and jumped to the side, freeing up the doorway. "Hope you aren't frozen solid. Come in! Come in! Welcome to Ruby's Place." She held the door open, hoping her smile helped thaw the bright pink ears and noses of her new

259

customers.

How long was she supposed to hold the door? She wasn't sure. But her head was still tumbling and the cold felt soothing, and she certainly didn't mind at all standing in place, watching the seemingly endless line of happy faces pass by.

"You trying to take my job?" Rob teased her. He winked, taking up his spot at the door. "Go on, go on. These folks want drinks."

Angela nodded. Her legs felt weak as she dipped behind the bar. "So far, so good," she told herself.

By the time she reached for her first glass, the entire pub had erupted in an incessant buzz—*hellos* and *old place looks just like I remembered*s and *let's get a table*s.

The high school music teacher plopped onto the piano bench and began to play a few chords. The crowd flowed toward her. And suddenly, carols filled the air.

Angela loaded a tray with cocoa and Ruby's famous homemade marshmallows. She watched Geena grab it up and try to make her way across a crowded bar.

As she walked, she was peppered with shouts of, "So good to see you and Rob together again!" Each of them loud enough to rise above the carols, the squeals, and to travel all the way to Angela.

"Again?" Justin echoed. "What do they mean, 'again'?"

He squinted first at Geena and then at his father. He'd arrived with a little blond girl all dressed up and fighting her heels. She was a shy thing, clutching onto his hand, avoiding eye contact with anyone who might try to say hello. Her fingers kept roving to her chin, as though checking on the large blemish she'd attempted to cover with a glob of makeup. Unfortunately, she was touching the blemish so much, the makeup was smudging and a shiny red lump was beginning to show through.

"Rob!" someone shouted, tossing a bough of mistletoe like a football.

Rob caught it as the crowd cheered.

"Kiss!" a voice cried out from the back of the room.

"What is this, a frat party?" Geena shouted. But she tossed her empty try on the nearest table, and Rob grabbed her in a bear hug. He dipped her overdramatically and kissed her, to cheers and applause.

"Satisfied now?" Geena called, waving her arms while Rob bowed theatrically.

"What gives?" Justin shouted at his dad. "And here you were giving me grief about Sarah."

Rob only wrapped an arm around Justin's neck while the rest of the bar exploded in laughter.

A chorus of well wishes directed toward the old sweethearts ended with various renditions of "Knew it all along…"

And "…you two were always meant to be together." And "…permanent as that old sidewalk square out there."

Ruby slammed her hands on her hips and eyed Angela in a *told you so* way.

Angela laughed as she poured another round. Ruby was right—Rob and Geena had done a better job of drawing a crowd than any fancy print ad or a drink special or even some big-name opening night entertainment ever could.

Geena had started to fill her tray again when a woman approached, introducing herself as the girl she'd once babysat. "Kimberly? Kimberly Tan?" Geena repeated with glee. The two women chatted, catching up, until Kimberly leaned in and said, "So weird. Have you seen that there's no snow on your names out there? The rest of the sidewalk got totally covered by the plow. Not your inscription, though. Almost like *Rob & Geena 4Ever* is so hot, snow melts as soon as it hits."

Geena rolled her eyes, but she turned her face toward the window, as though wondering if it were true. "Can't be," she muttered. "Has to be another bit of Sullivan gossip."

"You want a breather?" Angela shouted in her ear. "It's all got to be overwhelming."

"No way," Geena shouted back. And smiled. "This is the best I've felt in—well—since—"

Angela nodded in understanding.

"So weird how excited everyone is," Geena continued. "I doubted anyone around even remembered me and Rob."

"Maybe," Angela said, "other people can see our own happy endings before we do. Maybe we're too close to see it all. Maybe others have the kind of distance that lets them see the big picture."

Geena thought about that for a moment. "Maybe," she agreed. "Why? What do you see?"

Geena clearly thought she was still talking about Rob. And now, she was asking if Angela thought they were one of those fated couples, the kind whose story had been written in the stars—not just the sidewalk.

But that wasn't what Angela had been referring to—not entirely, anyway. "Look over there," she said, gesturing toward a handsome man standing by the piano. A man in a tweed jacket, with an old-fashioned but incredibly familiar mustache. He smiled and waved, greeting Geena warmly.

Angela stopped breathing. Everything was riding on this moment. Here it was—the true test. Would Geena even see him? Recognize him? Would Ruby's officially become the place Angela'd spent the past year hoping it would be?

Or would Geena simply frown, shrug, see nothing out of the ordinary, have no idea what Angela'd been trying to say?

Angela felt her whole life in the balance, suddenly.

Please, please, please, she thought. *Please, Geena. Do you see him?*

Geena touched the side of her face. Her mouth drooped in shock.

"Dad," Geena whispered.

43.

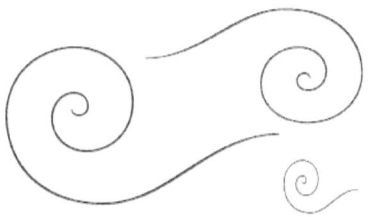

TOM motioned for Geena to join him in the back corner of the bar.

She raced to follow him, sliding into a tiny table for two, barely feeling the chair beneath her.

"Dad," she whispered. "Dad! You're here! How is this possible?"

"Don't question it, sweetie. Be grateful."

He looked exactly like he had when she was little—the summer of Mrs. Cranston and baking and learning that even when it felt like the world had crumbled, it hadn't, not really. After her parents' divorce, she'd simply begun to split her time between her mother's house and her father's. Life continued on. It was different, but it hadn't stopped. In the end, nothing had literally been destroyed. It had just kind of changed color.

"I'm so lonesome in the house without you," she said, wiping tears from her cheek. "I always thought of that house as my home. More than Mom's place. Maybe because that was where we were living when I was born. But mostly, I think, because you were there. Nothing could ever happen to me in your house. I was always safe."

Her father smiled at her. "I know. I kept the house—even though it was more than I really needed—because it was your home base. It's yours now, honey. It was always yours. But don't feel like you have to stay there. It's yours to do with as you choose. Do what's right for you. If that means selling it, then sell it. Your life is elsewhere now, and you shouldn't feel obligated to keep the old place because you want to feel close to me. I'm not there anymore."

"Maybe I do want it. The house."

He reached across the table and squeezed her hand. "Geena—"

"I'm here with Rob," she interrupted. "Is that what you wanted? Were you trying to get us together?" She rambled, words gushing. "You sent me out there. To The Page Turner. Right? You wanted me to see him."

"Geena, Geena." He was shaking his head adamantly.

"What? Did I get that wrong? I couldn't have. You insisted. And you knew—you knew he owned it. You wanted me with him. Didn't you?"

"I've come to believe, after all this time, that those

feelings between the two of you weren't youthful nonsense," Tom said. "I should have seen it before. Father's fear, I guess. I couldn't sit around and let you make a mistake you might wind up regretting. A mistake that could change the course of your life."

"I thought maybe it was something like that," Geena blubbered. She was shaking now. "But I was so unsure. Ever since you left, I've felt so unanchored. It's rattled me so much, knowing I don't have you to talk to anymore."

"Oh, hon—whatever happens next...I'll be glad, Geena, whatever it is, if it makes you happy. But I don't want you to feel like it has to be Rob because I sent you out there. Don't think I was trying to tell you who to love. Who to marry. If to marry. You don't need me to make good life choices. You can do that fine on your own."

"So you—"

"Rob grew into a really good man. I'll admit it. Better than I would have believed when you two were kids. And you've grown into a great woman. You were happy with him once. And I had you and Rob on my mind because—well." He paused, letting a smile etch itself into his cheek. "Look, when I was about the age you are now, love came to me a second time."

"I know—I mean, I just found out."

"You did?" Tom seemed honestly shocked. But his face

quickly relaxed as he said, "Good. I'm glad. I hated leaving with a secret like that between us. Look, Geena, sometimes, love does come again. It can come right when you've decided to go it alone. The woman I met, she was older than me, even. It happens, Geena. It does. If you're open to it. I was a little afraid you'd started to think you'd outgrown it. I thought maybe, by seeing Rob again, you would remember how great real love can feel. I thought it'd open you up to the possibility. Love isn't only for the young."

Geena grinned. "I figured it out. Who she was. I know about you and Mrs. Cranston."

Her father frowned. "Me and—?"

"Mrs. Cranston. Right? She kind of spilled the beans when she came by the house the other day."

"What, exactly, did she spill the beans about?" Now, he had the same serious look he'd once worn when questioning her about the dent in the fender or demanding she turn the music down.

"About—what you were just talking about. Right? You had a girlfriend. And didn't want me to know when I was little. Poor Mrs. Cranston. As soon as she started telling me about your girlfriend, she got so embarrassed…"

Her dad threw his head back and laughed.

"What? Why are you laughing?"

But Tom couldn't stop. He wrapped his arms around his ribs, like he was having to hold himself together.

"What? Dad!"

"It wasn't Mrs. Cranston," he said between snorts and guffaws, still trying to stop laughing.

"It wasn't? But she was so upset. And she said—she had some brooch that she said reminded her of you—"

"I probably gave it to her for Christmas to thank her for being so good to you. She was a godsend."

"But she wasn't—?"

"No," he said. "It was a woman I met out of the blue on a police call. Attempted robbery."

"Of her house?"

"Her business. And when I got there, I found out she'd actually already cornered the guy. I still don't know how she'd managed it, but he was tied to the checkout counter."

"With what?"

"Pantyhose." He was laughing harder now, all over again. And suddenly, so was Geena.

"Pantyhose!" she echoed.

"It was a women's dress shop," her dad continued. "Most successful shop in Sullivan. You shopped there a time or two with your mother, I'm sure."

"I still can't believe it," she said, putting her head in her hands. "You had someone. And you kept it secret! It was right there in front of me as I was growing up, and I never noticed."

Her father shrugged. "When a person truly wants to keep a secret, they can always find a way."

Geena's face clouded. "Stay awhile?" she whispered, hoping his own phrase might somehow convince him.

He glanced down at the tablecloth, digging his thumbnail into the fabric.

"Guess I need to take that as a no," Geena said. She leaned forward, clasping his hands. "If you can't, then I need— to tell you so many things."

"Oh, hon, you don't. I know—"

"No," Geena interrupted. "I want to tell you again how safe I always felt with you. Not just in the house. Anywhere you were was a safe place for me. I guess really, that's what dads are supposed to do for their kids. But you should know how wonderful everything was. Even when we fought about—stupid things. Boys. I wanted you to know how much I've missed you since you left and—how none of these words are enough. They're not, because…"

His raised his eyes to meet hers. "I know, sweetie. I love you, too. Always."

A moment of calm settled between them.

"Yeah," Geena said, tears filling her eyes. "I love you,

Dad."

She felt his hands sliding away, out of her grasp.

He stood, crossing to the other side of the table. Geena wiped her eyes before standing. She hugged him tighter than she ever had, not wanting to let go.

"Remember—love isn't for the young," Tom repeated, taking Geena's face in his hands. "Believe that."

He let go of her, looking at a distant point somewhere behind Geena's shoulder.

Geena swiveled.

A woman stood just a few feet away, looking straight at Tom: Well-coiffed, shoulder-length blond hair. Dark red lipstick. A mid-calf silky gray dress with a boat neck and three-quarter-length sleeves. The full, pleated skirt and her wide leather belt emphasized a still-trim waist, though she was obviously older. Maybe fifty-five. Every bit the image of polish and poise.

Tom smiled. "Hello, Elizabeth," he said.

44.

CHRISTMAS morning was fast approaching. It slith-ered down the frozen sidewalk. And it pressed its face against the window of Ruby's Place.

But Christmas couldn't stay away, out in the cold. Christmas wouldn't shrug its shoulders and slink off. Not when it was already this close.

No, Christmas had a job to do.

So it slipped right inside Ruby's. And it glanced around, taking stock.

The air crackled, filling with wishes. Yes, Christmas could hear them all—every dream, every fantasy. Christmas didn't need a jolly guy in a red suit to get to the bottom of what each person needed and desired most.

Christmas could hear every single heart, could dance through every single head.

It was Christmas's time to shine, after all.

And the old pub was exactly the kind of establishment where Christmas planned to leave its mark—a mark that would continue to be felt all year long.

"It's been a while," Elizabeth said softly.

"It sure has," Tom agreed, wearing a smile that matched hers.

Christmas nudged him, slamming its shoulder against Tom's. He staggered forward a few steps, finding he suddenly had Elizabeth's hand in his own.

Christmas smiled; this was a wish decades in the making.

Angela burst through a storage room, her fingers looped around the necks of gin and vodka bottles.

"Too long," Tom told Elizabeth.

"Too long for what?" Angela asked.

But Tom wasn't talking to her. He didn't even know she was there. Nor was he aware that anyone else was still in the bar, either. Not anymore. Christmas knew that Tom had just seen the entire room vanish, with the exception of Elizabeth. The sound of glorious Christmas bells filled his ears with joy.

Elizabeth smiled; she heard them, too.

"Elizabeth?" Angela asked tentatively, surprise drawing a trail of goose bumps down her arms. Tom had been Elizabeth's love? All the time they'd spent planning Tom's celebration of life, fretting about Geena's feelings—and Elizabeth had never said a word. It must have been torture.

"I wasn't sure I should come," Elizabeth confessed, still looking only at the man she'd left behind. "I knew you'd be here for Geena. And maybe it wasn't my place—maybe I'd only intrude…"

"We already talked," Tom told Elizabeth. But it was Angela who clearly felt reassured.

"Geena said everything she needed to," Tom went on. "We both did. She knows I need her to let me go. That she can't hang on to me out of some sense of obligation."

Christmas smiled. Tom was right. Ruby's Place wasn't about clutching to a past that had already come and gone. It wasn't about ignoring today.

Angela edged through the bar, giving Elizabeth and Tom privacy.

"I was afraid, too," Elizabeth admitted to Tom. "'First love.' That was your final message. Maybe you had someone else on your mind. Someone—"

"Only the woman who used to tell me I was hers," Tom said through a grin. "A second-act first love."

Elizabeth raised her eyebrows as if to question his explanation.

"Okay, so maybe it wasn't all I had on my mind. I was thinking of Geena, too. But you were there. Clear as the day we met. I'm not sweet talking you with a bunch of empty words. You know me better than that. What were you really afraid of?"

"We might not have recognized each other," Elizabeth admitted.

"Not recognize?"

"People don't always look exactly like we remember."

"Not in here, Elizabeth. We both know that in Ruby's on this night, people see with their hearts. But that's how I always saw you. With my heart."

Elizabeth teared up. Tom shook his head at her. "That's not what bothered you, either. Was it?"

"I guess," Elizabeth said, "I was mostly scared I'd show up to find things weren't the same between us. I wasn't sure I could handle that."

The two stared at each other a moment before dissolving into laughter. The same way people always laughed at fears that had never come to pass.

"Is this the first time you've been in the bar since…?" Elizabeth asked. She wrinkled her nose and let out a distinctive, "Pfff," tossing aside her awkwardness. What was the need for it? This was Tom—the same Tom she had known all those years ago. She asked, as she might have asked when they first met, "How long have you been here tonight? Have I simply been walking by you?"

"A little while. And yes, you have," Tom smiled.

"I missed you? Why didn't you say something?"

"Probably should have tied you up with your old pantyhose." Tom winked.

Elizabeth tossed her head back, laughter coming out this time like the notes of a perfectly arranged melody.

At the piano, Evie leaned forward to whisper into the ear of Anna Osbourne, the current high school music teacher. Anna flinched, raising her hands from the keys.

When she put them back, she didn't return to carols.

Anna played the opening notes of an old song, a classic—one that Evie had urged her to play now. One that Anna's own piano instructor had given her to learn.

Piano lessons—those had been a Christmas present, too. From Anna's grandmother. Christmas remembered that one well.

The lilting melody of "I Remember You" wafted through the room. Anna played it flawlessly, though she hadn't thought of it in years. She couldn't quite figure out how she remembered the notes so clearly.

Christmas knew, though.

This was not the "I Remember You" that had once filled

the Caprice on a snowy Christmas Eve. Not the "I Remember You" Rob and Geena had listened to on the radio as she'd unwrapped her unforgettable hundredth Christmas gift.

This was Tom's favorite. The Johnny Mercer version. "I Remember You," that old standard about a reunion between two former lovers—how it had seemed mere kisses ago that they had parted.

Dorothy, the jazz singer who had once shared her vocals with the regulars at Ruby's, leaned against the edge of the piano and began to sing. As did all the rest of those in the crowd who remembered the lyrics. How well their voices blended. Christmas noticed—and approved of the pairing. Especially since many in the current Ruby's crowd could not hear the regulars at all. Christmas wanted everyone to hear the song, which carried with it the power of a second chance.

Humming along, Elizabeth erased the last centimeters of space between herself and Tom. "Feels like a first Christmas all over again," she observed. But this time around, there was no need to be careful. To try to keep a secret from Tom's young daughter. A girl hurt by his divorce, spending her holiday with her mother across town. They were free from all the gossipy taboos life had placed on them.

The mere kisses ago in which their dreams had come true were indeed a lifetime gone. But the ghost of their old love had already started to breathe all over again.

"I'd tell the angels you were my greatest thrill," Tom murmured into Elizabeth's ear, playing off the song's lyrics.

"I might've said something similar a time or two," Elizabeth whispered.

It was true; Christmas had heard it often.

On the other side of the room, Geena bumped into Rob. He swept her into his arms.

Immediately, Christmas dimmed the lights, turning the room as hazy as a dream coming into focus.

In the midst of the blur, Christmas began to grant wishes all across the bar. To be sure, Ruby and the regulars had made its work easy. All Christmas had to do was listen to the spirits, follow their instructions, let them lead the way. And suddenly, love was back, flowing in ways it hadn't, not for years. Love between parent and child, between first loves, late-in-life loves. But Christmas also brought the welcome release that had come to Geena after hearing her father ask that she live her own life. It renewed the admiration Angela'd felt for her aunt when she was a child, her desire to grow up to emulate her. It intensified the love that came to Angela now, seeing Elizabeth for the first time as a woman with her own hopes and dreams. Christmas continued to swirl through the room, salvaging friendships. Granting acceptance. Providing forgiveness.

Over and over, the past and present collided. Endings had not been endings at all, but merely a pause. A bookmark. Ruby's Place was suddenly home to *I miss you*s and *I'm sorry*s and *I love you still*s.

The heart, Christmas knew, was no fickle instrument. It was a safe whose combination was known only to the owner. Everyone in Ruby's Place was at that moment unlocking the emotions they'd stored away. Emotions that had never waned or diminished.

Not even when hearts stopped beating.

Love survived everything. It even survived life itself.

Tom and Elizabeth danced.

Rob and Geena danced.

Music swelled all around them.

Other customers—those who remained unaware of the regulars—continued on with their own celebrations. But Christmas wasn't ignoring them. Instead, it was making sure that this was not a single glittering evening but the start of a new tradition. A first time that would be forever etched into their own memories.

Christmas was already making sure they'd return next year—to Ruby's.

"...sure did breathe life back into the place..." The words repeatedly floated through the bar.

But Christmas knew that wasn't right. Life had always lain waiting inside Ruby's Place. The past had always been ready to reach out and touch the present. All anyone needed was an open heart. And a little belief in the magic of Christmas.

Through the plate glass window, the neon "Ruby's Place" sign glowed, casting a soft red light onto the snowflakes that fell softly around the edges of an old sidewalk square. And inside the storied walls, Ruby's customers—old and new—danced along the edge of forever.

45.

RUBY squealed as she burst outside to celebrate, her voice rippling down the alleyway.

"It worked!" she shouted to the constellations above, the snowflakes trickling onto her upturned face. "Oh, I believed. But even the strongest belief is laced with the teensiest bit of doubt. There was always a chance it wouldn't work. So many variables at play. And there's no telling about people. They can talk themselves out of miracles that are staring them square in the face."

She squealed again, fists raised triumphantly.

"And maybe it didn't happen all because of me, but I had quite the hand in it, didn't I?" Ruby bragged, twirling and striking the pose she had once reserved for encores during the height of her career. "I manipulated fridges and changed the course of events. Angela would be nowhere without me. I know how to draw the crowds and I know exactly how to get all the necessary ingredients together for the most powerful, intoxicating cocktail of all."

She clapped, laughing with utter delight.

A trill caught her attention.

A bright red cardinal had landed near her, in the alleyway, pecking at the crumbs of sugar cookies left behind by revelers. He stopped to look her way.

"Cardinals appear when angels are near," Ruby muttered. "Isn't that what Angela's always repeating, red bird?"

The cardinal cocked his head to the side and jumped forward a few steps.

"Not afraid of me, little guy? You want to talk? You want to ask me about this place of mine? Hmm? You want to know what just went on inside? My Christmas wish came true, that's what. Memories have floated back up to the top. The past has been resurrected. Yesterday and today have blurred.

"Ah, but then again, what is a ghost other than a memory that has come to life?" Ruby asked the cardinal, not waiting for an answer before continuing to question the red bird.

"Come clean—how old are you, fella? You have any memories of Ruby's Place yourself? Is that what drew you here? Has to be a reason. Isn't this kind of late for you to be out? Isn't there a nest somewhere with your name on it?"

The cardinal chirped at her as though to respond.

Ruby squinted, moving slightly closer. "*Is* there some bit of truth in Angela's favorite saying? You do have wings, after all."

The cardinal cocked his head to the other side.

"Not very talkative for an angel, are you?"

Still, the cardinal stared.

"Come on—quit this bird stuff. Let's get real with each other. We can do that. Look at us—what do we have to lose? Why should we have to pretend?"

A snowflake drifted to land on the cardinal's beak.

"Don't you think we should talk about our current circumstances—me seeing you, you seeing me?"

But the cardinal, appearing to find her question a bit too personal, ruffled his feathers and took to flight

He'd be back, though. Ruby was sure of it. All living beings—cardinals included—were nothing more than creatures of habit, after all.

"See you next year," Ruby called out, as he disappeared in the black night sky.

46.

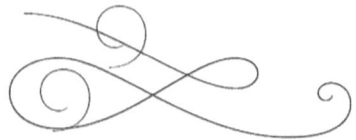

ROB was bruised and borderline tipsy. He figured he'd probably walked ten miles making the rounds back and forth across the bar, greeting and seating the constant stream of new customers.

Along the way, his ribs had been elbowed, his toes smashed, his shins whacked. Each time, the apology of choice had come in the form of a shot or a spiced ale. "On me!" the merrymaker would declare proudly.

He'd accepted too many. His head was swimming. His body felt oddly loose.

"Rob!" Angela shouted. "Help deliver a few dinners?"

He nodded, crashing and pinballing off customers as he made his way toward the kitchen, where he picked up several plates of holiday ham, lining the dishes down one arm.

Plunking the meals on a table, he smiled, wiped sweat

from his forehead. And found himself jumping into an emergency scoot to the side. But he didn't move quite fast enough to avoid being hit in the hip with a chair.

"So sorry," Susan Fitzweather's husband bellowed. "Let me get you—"

"No!" Rob shouted with a giggle. "No more."

He tried to stumble toward the bar, but his feet tangled and he crashed straight into another customer, who caught him and set him back on his feet.

"Thanks," Rob sighed, finding himself looking into a stern face, complete with a thick black mustache. He blinked. The guy was the mirror image of Tom—or the way he'd looked more than a couple dozen years ago, back when Rob was in high school. Then again, this guy seemed younger. Didn't he? This guy didn't have gray in his hair at all. Maybe Tom hadn't, either, when he'd started dating Geena. Maybe Rob had been the reason for those streaks.

Still, the guy was so similar, Rob instantly got that familiar dip in the stomach—the *oh, no* feeling that had usually accompanied seeing Tom back then.

"Took you thirty-*one* years to convince me. For the record." The man smiled, patted his shoulder, then turned toward his date and danced her away, all before Rob could make sense of any of it.

Such a strange thing to say. Who was he? And where had he gone?

Rob shook the encounter away and tapped the bar. "Can I get a cup of coffee?" he asked Angela.

She nodded, looking plenty frazzled herself, her hair falling from a haphazard ponytail and her own sweaty face blazing a bright flustered fuchsia.

As Rob leaned against the bar's edge, the lights flickered. Briefly—but enough to get a rolling "Booo" from the crowd.

Still. The flicker had tapped his memory. It came to him: Sitting alone with Tom at the Barister kitchen table. After Rob had been stranded by a snowstorm. In a power outage. Geena upstairs, searching for a board game. Rob defending the affection he felt for Geena to her disbelieving father. He had, in his best imitation of an adult voice, vowed to Tom that it would be perfectly fine if it took a full thirty years to convince him of what a sincere guy he was.

The Big One; that was when he'd had that conversation with Tom. During the awful storm back in December—of 1987.

Thirty-one years ago.

Rob's head bobbed up, and he tried desperately to search the crowd for Tom's face. But there were too many people, with far too little space between.

He began to catch snippets of conversation:

"…used to come here every year with my dad…"

"…I swear, it's all coming back to me…"

"…feel like I can still see him, standing near the bar…"

"…imagination can get the best of you in a place like this…"

Could it be true? Or, after what was clearly one too many drinks, had he simply made it all up? Was it nothing more than wishful thinking? What Rob hoped Tom would have said to him, given the chance?

All Rob knew for sure was that if Tom really had said such a thing to him, it would have been one of the most satisfying, unexpected Christmas gifts he'd ever received.

47.

THE night's pulse grew weaker. The crowds thinned. The tide of people began to flow in the opposite direction, back out the door.

Geena wiped down the tables in the darker corners herself. Her father was most assuredly not there. Nor was there any indication he had ever been.

Oh, Geena, come on, she told herself. Her dad visiting Ruby's so he could magically tell her everything she needed to hear? It was too absurd to even consider.

By that point, hours after her encounter with her father, the whole thing felt like a vivid daydream. Grief did strange things to the mind, she supposed.

And yet she felt so oddly peaceful.

Arms reached out from behind her to wrap around her waist. Geena twisted to find Rob standing behind her, smiling.

"Some kind of night," he said excitedly, pushing her

unruly blond hair behind her ear.

It had been. It might have been. It...

Geena smiled at him in agreement. No "mights" about it. She was with Rob. And they'd been part of an amazing opening night for Angela. One for the record books, surely.

"Where'd Justin get to?" Geena asked.

"Took Sarah home a couple of hours ago. Curfew."

"Might remember something about those."

The cooks were gone, too. And the last of the dirty dishes. So much preparation, and now, they were left with the strange buzzy stillness that settled into a space right after a burst of activity.

Angela appeared from behind the bar and began shoving money at both of them. They protested, their mini fight of sorts occurring amid protests of, "It's Christmas! Let me!" from Angela, and "It's Christmas! We wanted to help!" from Rob and Geena.

"Promise the two of you will come back to the place—not to work—to enjoy a good meal and a special evening."

Rob and Geena agreed. Hugs were exchanged. "Goodnight"s circled through the air.

Angela thanked them again before turning her "Closed" sign to face the street. Rob and Geena found themselves on the sidewalk, the snowflakes swirling between them.

"So," Rob said, "*are* you staying in Sullivan—or going back?"

"I'm not selling the house." She couldn't bear the thought of not having the old home base.

"Does that mean you're—"

"—here for good?" Geena finished. "I'm going back to teach next semester. I have a contract. But I'll be here in the summer. In the future? Who knows."

"I'll keep a shelf in The Page Turner waiting for you," Rob promised.

"Deal," Geena whispered.

Footsteps drew their attention down the sidewalk.

Scott Drummond offered a kind of embarrassed, awkward wave. "Looks like we're down to the last men standing," he joked.

"Where's the rest of the family?" Rob asked.

"Home," Scott said, pointing behind his shoulder. "The kids, you know—they were wiped out. Needed to go to bed, so I dropped them and my wife off."

"Why'd you come back?" Geena asked.

Scott shrugged. "I remembered it all so fondly. And it made me feel so—I don't know—close to the old times that..."

"That what?" Geena pressed.

"I wanted to come in case maybe people were still here.

I was hoping I hadn't missed everyone. But it's wound down now, hasn't it?"

"Yeah, Angela's already locked up," Rob said.

Scott's breath made clouds as he turned his face toward the warm red neon sign. "Funny thing—my dad used to bring me here when I was a kid. And tonight, for some reason…"

Geena stopped breathing.

Scott laughed at himself. "The Christmas spirit can get to you, I guess."

He started to back up. "I should really go home. Technically, Christmas Eve is over. Merry Christmas, you two."

"Merry Christmas," Geena echoed, her heart aching to ask him a hundred questions. Had he seen something? Could he tell her something that would let her believe her talk with her father had been real?

Rob squeezed her hand as a way to pull her attention from Scott's dwindling figure.

Should she ignore Rob for the moment? Call out to Scott? Ask him what he'd seen? Demand from the universe that it provide some sort of proof, one way or another, about what had happened that night with her father?

In the end, Geena let Scott go without another word. Some things, she thought, were almost better left uncertain.

"Do you know how especially wonderful Christmas

morning is at Dad's house?" Geena asked.

"Do I get to find out?" Rob asked, leading her toward his truck.

Only a few steps away, they paused near their old sidewalk square.

Rob & Geena 4Ever.

48.

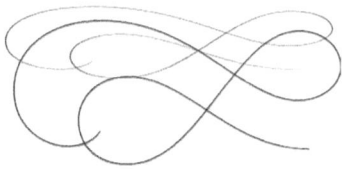

MEANWHILE, a cluster of shadowy faces remained in the window, watching: Angela, Ruby, Elizabeth, Tom, and Walter.

"We did it," Walter murmured. "We really did it."

"You and Tom," Angela repeated, shaking her head at her aunt. "That's what I can't believe."

"Pfff," Elizabeth said, dismissing her niece with a toss of the hand. "You've only begun to finally see the tip of the iceberg." She winked, her eyes sparkling.

"Nobody said anything," Tom marveled. "About what they saw. Not even Geena?"

"No," Ruby agreed. "I didn't think they would."

"Everybody protects their own secrets," came a low call from the back.

The five of them turned, finding two figures still seated at a table. Roy Weber flicked his gold lighter, firing up a fresh

Pall Mall. "Your own secrets," Roy said around the cigarette, "are something you never gossip about. Not ever. If my wife hadn't already left, she'd tell you the same."

"Who is that?" Angela whispered into Ruby's ear.

Ruby narrowed her eyes and crossed her arms over her chest.

"Oh, don't get all upset," Roy grumbled, pulling himself from his chair. "I lost a bet. Long time ago." He pointed at Nick, who was still downing the last of his beer.

"Great night, Ruby," Nick said. "A rousing success. Like always."

Roy made a face, causing the small group at the window to burst into satisfied laughter.

"Do I get to hear this story?" Angela asked Ruby as Roy and Nick disappeared from the bar.

"It's a long one," Ruby warned.

"I have time." Angela reached to turn off the neon "Ruby's Place" sign.

No need to keep washing the sky red, she thought. The sunrise would be coming along soon enough.

49.

FOUR MONTHS LATER

THREE children skipped down the sidewalk toward Ruby's. They crackled with sugar energy, having emerged from a new ice cream shop down the street. Their parents lingered near the entrance, talking in their boring adult way.

Outside Ruby's door, the children stopped. To two of them, Ruby's seemed out of bounds—maybe even a touch spooky. Especially now that it was closed up tight and dark inside, no business on Sunday.

One little girl—reaching her hand out, obviously trying to work up the courage to put her fingertips on the bright green door—spoke up as if an authority on the place. "My mom says weird things happen in there."

"Like what?" the boy asked, crinkling his nose at the dark front window.

"I dunno," she answered. "Just weird."

"Not weird. Magical. That's what *my* mom says," piped up the other little girl. She tossed her braid behind her shoulder with a flourish.

"I wish I could go inside," the little boy moaned.

"I'm going," the girl with the braid announced, weaving her fingers together behind her back and sticking her chest out. "Next Christmas Eve. Mom promised she'd take me."

"Lucky," the boy whispered.

"Maybe we can take you." The girl with the braid squinted, cupping her hands around her eyes as she stood on her tiptoes and tried to peer inside the window.

"Christmas Eve," she moaned. Why did it have to be so far away? Two or three lifetimes, it seemed to her. The mystery surrounding Ruby's Place was itchy. She needed to get her fingers into it.

Her friends quickly lost interest. Having given up on the locked door and black windows, they skipped down the sidewalk in the opposite direction, back toward their parents.

"Hey, wait!" she shouted.

She let go of the windowsill. But before she raced after

her friends, she whispered, "I'm coming back. I'm going to find out what's inside."

She didn't know it, but on the other side of the glass, a hazy face smiled back. "See you then, sweet girl."

A promise made—one to be kept during another magical Christmas Eve at Ruby's Place.

COME BACK TO RUBY'S PLACE

I Remember You is the second installment in the Ruby's Place Christmas Series:

Find out how it all started with **Christmas at Ruby's**, the prequel to **I Remember You**.

The speakeasy days come back to Sullivan in **Sentimental Journey**, the third installment in the series.

In the finale to the Ruby's Place series, readers are given the ultimate Christmas gift, as they discover for themselves the truth about Christmas Eve in this special nightspot.

Look for the full series Ebook, which includes all four books in a single download.

CHECK HOLLYSCHINDLER.COM FOR AVAILABILITY

HOLLY SCHINDLER is an award-winning and critically acclaimed author of books for readers of all ages. She firmly believes that nothing is quite as magical as a good story or an exciting new "what-if." She is currently chasing down her next "what-if" as she writes her next book. She also loves hearing from her readers. If you'd like to get in touch or subscribe to her newsletters, please visit her online at:

HOLLYSCHINDLER.COM